Send One Angel Down

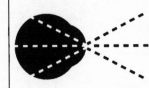

This Large Print Book carries the
Seal of Approval of N.A.V.H.

Send One Angel Down

Virginia Frances Schwartz

Thorndike Press • Waterville, Maine

Copyright © 2000 by Virginia Frances Schwartz

All rights reserved.

The writing of this novel was supported, in part, by a grant from the Society of Children's Book Writers and Illustrators.

Published in 2003 by arrangement with Holiday House.

Thorndike Press Large Print Young Adult Series.

The tree indicium is a trademark of Thorndike Press.

The text of this Large Print edition is unabridged.
Other aspects of the book may vary from the original edition.

Set in 16 pt. Plantin by Christina S. Huff.

Printed in the United States on permanent paper.

ISBN 0-7862-4800-9 (lg. print : hc : alk. paper)

For my mother

"Yesterday, a night-gone thing
a sun-down name."[*]

[*]from *Time of Trial, Time of Hope* by M. Meltzer and
A. Meier 1966 / Doubleday

The writing of this novel was supported, in part, by a grant from the Society of Children's Book Writers and Illustrators.

This novel is based
on a true story
about a slave
named Eliza as told
by her cousin
Abram.

If-a you can't come,
If-a you can't come, Lord,
Send-a one angel down.
Send him on a rainbow,
Send him in a glory,
Send him in a hurry, Lord,
If-a you can't come.

Contents

1846–1860

Chapter 1

Ring Them Bells

She was born after me, six years to be exact. That's how Eliza and I kept time, by each other's born days.

I crouched by the door of the breeding cabin that long April night Aunt Charity waited to give birth to Eliza.

"Master promised me, Abram," my aunt had told me. "I get to keep my firstborn child. Boy or girl, it don't matter. Won't be sold away like the others that come. You will have a cousin soon."

If she lived.

My aunt was a plump, brown woman of eighteen. Smiles lit her face like sunbeams most of the time, but I was worried through and through that night. It was her first child. That's how it was when my momma birthed me. I don't remember her, for she died just as I was born, there in that breeding cabin.

"Too young, your momma was," recalled Granny. "Thirteen years old and string-bean thin. Prettiest girl on the plantation, but she up and left us all."

I lived with Aunt Charity and Granny these six years.

She wasn't my real granny. Granny was just a name folks called her. Her skin was dark as the night sky. Hair wiggled out from her kerchief like snakes. She was hard and shut tight like a walnut shell. She cawed around the yard, barking orders bold as a crow. She never gave me smiles like Aunt Charity.

Granny always wore boots, black leather, lace-up boots that Master bought her. None of us ever owned such a thing. She was so proud of those boots, she stamped down hard in 'em so we all heard her coming.

Granny was the boss of the breeding cabins, which meant she delivered all the babies. Breeding slaves made a lot of money for the Master. Some babies were sold off at auction. Some stayed to work the cotton fields. Either way, owning us slaves made Master rich.

I was Granny's running boy. I owed her for the job. It was better than sweating in the fields and hauling cotton. I wasn't sold away like all the rest either.

"Need a boy child to help me," she demanded of Master the day I was born. "Babies swarmin' around here like flies."

Master must have looked at me, kicking up a storm in her arms, then down at my momma, her eyes shut tight. Maybe, I thought when I heard the story, just maybe, he had made the same promise to my momma as he made to Aunt Charity. *You can keep your firstborn child.* He nodded at Granny, and I got to stay.

She was the one who named me Abram. No one else around to do it. Aunt Charity was still a child then, and my daddy was a runaway. He up and left before I was born, Granny told me. Never even knew I was coming.

I was Granny's shadow around the breeding cabins. About twenty breeders lived there, and they kept Granny and me running. Granny brooded over 'em like a rooster over a flock of hens. She coaxed 'em through deliveries and their babies' colic both. Sometimes a woman bled too early. She'd have to lie flat down and not move 'til her baby came. Granny stuffed small green potatoes into her pockets to cure cramping. Once a baby came in a breeder's fifth month. It was so tiny, it fit into Granny's hand. It never took a breath.

On birthing nights, I fetched water from the mile-back stream and boiled it over a fire. Then I passed steaming water buckets inside. I paced outside on the porch that long April night, passing buckets inside, waiting for Granny to call me. But there was no word. I squatted by the fire awhile. Fire twisted in and out of the sticks. I couldn't keep my eyes off 'em. Flames danced all over those sticks, licking them up, swallowing 'em whole.

A burlap sack was nailed over the breeding cabin window, but it was softly lit inside. Only on birthing nights did Granny get a candle to burn. Shadows darkened the burlap. Granny shuffled back and forth with buckets and rags. Her black boots were tap-tap-tapping beside the straw mat where my aunt lay. There was moaning and groaning from Aunt Charity. I listened until I couldn't bear any more, then stirred up the fire to heat more buckets. But soon enough, I'd be peeking beneath the door again like a mouse.

Ten buckets I had passed inside, and still there was no word. By midnight, I stretched out on the porch. I tapped my fingers on the wood to pass the time. I'd seen men drum on hollow tree stumps around the quarters before. I must have banged down hard on

16

those boards, for Granny soon stomped to the door to hush me.

I hung my head down and carved pictures into the porch wood with a sharp willow stick next. I made pictures of cotton buds cracking the boll wide open and sunrays so hot they scorched the Alabama ground. I drew fifty cabins standing all in a row, slave quarters, sitting a flat mile behind the white plantation house. Master's house was big enough for a hundred white folks, but it held only four. House slaves lived there too, I heard, dressed in stiff aprons and shoes. An orchard sprung up between the big house and the cabins like heavenly grace. Maybe I dozed some, but not long.

Round dawn, I jerked up.

"H-o-o ah hoo!" someone wailed far off in the morning fog, so I could not see him.

"H-o-o ah hoo! H-o-o ah hoo!" came the answer. It groaned like someone with a toothache pulsing at night, sure there'd be no end to the pain. It sounded as mournful as death.

I sat straight up, shaking from head to toe.

"H-o-o ah hoo!" called one voice in the darkness.

"H-o-o ah hoo!!" a chorus of voices answered it.

I had never seen 'em up close. The first

time I heard such singing before, I'd been up all night with the whooping cough. I had peeked out the window in the fog and saw shadows float across the quarters. I whispered to Granny that ghosts were coming by.

"It's just the field workers walkin' through the slave quarters," she shushed me. "Voices ringin' out like a gong to awaken everyone — don't be caught asleep in the quarters after daybreak!"

Beneath me, the ground trembled. Voices hummed louder and louder. They were moving closer. I curled into a tight ball. The leader stepped out of the fog, wearing a shred of cloth for a shirt, like a veil over his bones. He looked older than Granny and stared straight ahead. One by one, men and women stumbled behind him. There were a hundred in all, chanting that song like it was a chain linking them tight together. They marched in tune with it.

"Hoo ah h-o-o! Hoo-o-o ah h-o-o!"

Not one of them saw me, I sat so still. They heaved hoes across their shoulders and disappeared in the mist, headed toward the cotton fields.

That's when the crows saved me. They passed by, screaming high above my head. *Caw! Caw! Caw!* Just two of 'em flying side by side, black wings beating the sky. Now, you hardly ever see just two of 'em. Mostly you see a flock. Two's luck, my aunt once told me. Then from inside the cabin came such a stir, I scrambled to my feet. Such a hollering! A newborn was screeching loud that it had come, and Aunt Charity was laughing and crying at the same time. I guess they forgot all about me waiting outside, so I banged hard on that door with both fists until Granny let me in.

Aunt Charity lay with the baby in her arms, cheeks shiny, smiling right through her tears. She hummed a glory tune beneath her breath.

> *Go ring them bells!*
> *I heard from Heav-en to-day.*
> *Go ring them bells!*

"Come here, Abram. You hear those two crows?" She invited me inside. "They announcin' good luck is comin' out of all our troubles. Here she is! I promised myself if it's a girl, her name will be Eliza. We got to be believin', boy. Even in hard times, there's good too."

I sucked in my breath. Eliza was my gone-away mother's name.

"Take off that long face," she chided me.

"Got us a girl child. Looks just like your momma. Isn't she a beauty?"

The light at the window was gray, and I blinked hard to see. I crept up close to the baby. She was such a tiny thing to fill your eye, smooth and naked from top to toe, long legged. Black hair pressed flat and wet to her head.

"Go ahead, boy." My aunt smiled. "Touch her."

When I petted the top of Eliza's head, her eyes popped open, big and blue as the sky. I remembered Granny telling me how sometimes babies were born like that, with blue eyes changing to brown in a few months. But even before the light grew bright, I knew Eliza'd have troubles. Granny tapped one foot down hard, her hands on her hips, staring out the window toward the big house. She wasn't laughing and crying with Aunt Charity and me. Her mouth turned down in bitter lines like she tasted something sour.

When the morning light shone bright through the window, I could finally see Eliza. Her skin was creamy like milk that's not been stirred into coffee yet but just sits on top, the brown kind of sinking in.

"Master's her father," Granny muttered. "Master Turner, owner of us all."

Some folks are closed up tight as a drum. When the Master stared at us slaves, his eyes were blank like he didn't see anything but field and sky. He had two white daughters up at that big house. He didn't want Eliza. All he wanted was more slaves to pick the three hundred acres of cotton on his plantation.

When a child was born to a slave mother, that child was a slave too, no matter who the father was. It didn't matter if he was a slave or if he was Master Turner.

Chapter 2

Come, Butter, Come

Early next morning, Aunt Charity set to work spinning piles of cotton into thread. For one month after delivery, breeders did light work, so my aunt wasn't cooking breakfast for the field slaves as usual. She wrapped her newborn in a dishcloth and handed her to me before sunup. I was sound asleep, curled up in a corner of the breeding cabin.

"Take care of Eliza, Abram. Carry her back to me for feedin' but do all the chores Granny sets for you," instructed my aunt. "Watch her close now."

I held the bundle that was Eliza stiff in my arms at first. I'd never been alone with a baby before. My legs shook. I stepped on tiptoe. I was breathless careful.

Outside in the yard, the breeding women were busy. Those in their early months hoed

Master's garden or tended the chickens and ducks. Annie Mae's daughter, Tempie, had just killed a turkey and was plucking his feathers clean off for Master's dinner. She nodded good morning but didn't dare pause in her work. Susie and Hannah sat quietly on chairs mending cloth. Their bellies were swollen tight as plums. Soon they'd be birthing their babies. Master didn't allow 'em to lift or bend.

I slipped past Granny standing by the butter churn. Milk had just been poured into it, so I knew she'd be busy awhile. She wouldn't have any chores to bother me with right away. She had her face squeezed up, eyes shut tight, humming low. She was working a spell. She said the devil puts a charm on milk so that it won't do what you want. Only chanting and churning could make the butter come. She believed the devil's the reason we all were slaves too, but so far no amount of her chanting had set us free.

Behind my back, I heard the spell song.

> *Come, but-ter, come!*
> *The King an' the Queen*
> *are a-stand-in' at the gate*
> *wait-in' for some but-ter*
> *and a cake.*
> *Oh come, but-ter, come!*

I headed back to the cabin where I lived with Aunt Charity and Granny. Sometimes my aunt would come home so late I fell asleep waiting for her. But it was mostly empty in the daytime when both of 'em were off working. I laid that child against my chest the way I had seen Granny do and sat down with her. I rocked Eliza for hours that first morning. Everything about her was tiny: ten tan fingers, ten coffee toes. Breath puffed in and out of her chest, which was no bigger than a bird's. Pump. Pump. Pump. It was like we were the only two folks in the world, Eliza and me.

It seemed a whole year had passed by when I heard Granny holler, "Where is that boy? We're needin' water to soak this dried corn for dinner, and he's nowhere to be found!"

I poked my head out the cabin window. The handle on Granny's churn stood straight up so that I knew the butter had come. The sun was high in the sky. All morning, I sat baby watching. I'd never been still a moment in my life unless I was asleep. I hopped here and there like a leapfrog. Granny yelled "Go!" and I jumped. For the first time, I had forgotten my chores.

Just when I stood up, Eliza woke with such a howling, they must have heard it all around the plantation. I shot like a streak of lightning past Granny who was dropping her jaw and waving a wooden spoon at me, straight to Eliza's mother.

Aunt Charity owned one pink calico dress that was always crisp and clean. Her collar was smooth and her face freshly scrubbed. She was always singing songs she learned in church, glory songs that made her smile. The harder she worked, the louder she sang. Her voice rang out like a bell tolling across the yard into my ears.

I turn my eyes to-ward the sky.
Ask the Lord for wings to fly.
If you get there be-fore —

She broke off when she saw us. She straightened up from scooping dinner out of the feeding trough, her palms pressed deep into her back.

"That's nothin' but a hunger cry is all." She laughed. "Hand her over to me."

Aunt Charity sat right down in the dirt and nursed Eliza. It was not the first time I saw such a thing. Babies were born on the plantation every month.

Eliza fed with both fists clenched, face scrunched up, her whole body aching for milk. Maybe I shouldn't have let her sleep so long, I told myself. Next time, I promised, I wouldn't let her get so hungry.

All the first months with Eliza passed like that. I flew back and forth from Aunt Charity to the river, then bent over the feeding trough and stirred up grits for Granny. Eliza was strapped to my chest with a strip of old horse blanket so I could watch her face to face. If she even wiggled a toe, I felt it poking against me.

When I couldn't stop her crying, I'd bang on the trough with a big wooden stick. I mixed up a beat to one of Granny's spell songs as I stirred grits. *Tap! Tap! Tap!* Eliza would gasp and look down at the racket. Soon enough, she'd be smiling.

It got to be I knew when she was hungry too, because her blue eyes dimmed a minute before she cried. Seconds later, I'd be at Aunt Charity's side, handing Eliza over.

"You fussin' over this girl child so," she joked, "think you are the mother!"

She threw back her head of curls and laughed. When Aunt Charity laughed, her curls laughed too. Every night she tied her hair up with strips of rags, and next day, the curls sat tight on top her head. They shook when her big body shook. She didn't laugh at me the way some did, teasing me for being slow.

Folks said I had a hangdog look. I couldn't help it. My mind was full of so many lonesome things at once. I didn't smile much either. When my aunt laughed, she was trying her best to make me laugh too.

Eliza gurgled at us, full of warm milk in that fat tummy of hers. She threw her head back just like Aunt Charity and laughed too. My aunt howled at the two of us. I was the last to let go. I whooped along with them, bellyaching. I'd been crowing over Eliza like some bossy old rooster.

Laughter's like light. It fills the night with a shine like stars. It brightened our cabin more than all the lamps in the big house at Christmastime. Eliza was the good that had come out of all our troubles, just like Aunt Charity said.

Chapter 3

Ask the Lord for Wings to Fly

Slave mothers got fed full up when they were with child. Long as they were nursing too, they were fed from the big house, not from the slave trough with the field workers. Aunt Charity was eating meat every day with chunks of cheese and fresh milk. She was plump around her hips, and round-faced too.

She had birthed two healthy boys since Eliza but brought none home to stay with us. Master sold such babies away. Boys brought the highest price at auction those days. Sometimes babies were sold off before they were weaned. If it was time for the monthly auction, Master didn't wait, no matter how much their mommas screamed. I could hear 'em weeping in the cabins when the overseer took their babies. It was like somebody died. But I never heard my aunt cry. She tiptoed about her work so quiet like she wasn't even there.

Firstborn children stayed on the plantation. They'd work the fields someday or become breeders like Tempie. Twin babies were born in Tempie's first birthing when she was seventeen. Everyone, even the field workers, ran in to see 'em. We all believed twins were lucky, but these ones weren't. The newborns wore the same face 'cept one was tiny and the other had a strong cry. Tempie had to choose — one to keep, one to sell. Two days passed. Tempie couldn't decide. She wouldn't let go of the small one for he'd need tending to live. But if she kept him, he might die anyway, and then she'd have nothing.

On the third day, Master stomped into the cabin.

"Which one came out first?" he demanded of Granny.

"The strong one." Granny pointed.

"He's firstborn," Master thundered. "He stays!"

We never knew if the small one lived. Tempie wandered around lost in thought most days after that. Granny had to nudge her to nurse the one baby she had left.

She didn't have to nudge Aunt Charity and me to care for Eliza though. That child was all we thought about. She was the only one who could make my aunt smile.

But one day, I heard Granny fuss to my aunt, my ear pressed to the door of the breeding cabin. "Master says the nursin's got to stop now that your child is two years old," she grumbled, "just when she's gettin' ready to grow. Got too many scrawny kids starvin' around here already."

Eliza was running barefoot by then, always heading off somewhere like an ant. When I scooped her up, her dimpled legs wiggled in all directions, still traveling the same old trail.

I burst in on the breeding cabin with her in my arms.

"I know where to get some food," I announced. "Up at the big house. House slaves get extra. They could save a bite for Eliza."

Stories passed around about Master eating meat every day. House slaves said there were bowls of ripe fruit everywhere. I had never dared to run up there before, never begged for a bite myself. My aunt nodded her head at me, but Granny cussed.

"House slaves cut from different cloth than us!" she cawed. "They dance to Master's tune. Obey all he says."

"We gotta do as Master says too, Granny."

30

"We got to do it, boy, but we don't like it!" Granny raised her fist at me. "That's the difference between us and house slaves. They think Master is God, but he's the devil!"

Soon a change came to the big house. Everyone was talking about the new nanny Master bought at auction. They said she was young. Maybe she would help me.

One morning, I woke Granny early before she went off to the breeding cabin. Everyone was still asleep on the dirt floor. I took a deep breath first.

"What about askin' the white girls' new nanny for food? She got to have a soft spot for young 'uns. That's her job."

"That one!" Granny screeched like a mad crow. "She's a Creole. Brought up in Louisiana, all fancy as you please. Miss Layotte they call her. Got French blood and a stiff collar. Think she's gonna help you? Come from the devil, that girl."

"I could just ask her," I insisted.

"You show up at her door beggin'," hissed Granny, "and she'll tell Master. Sure as sure, be a whippin' later. Stay away from her, boy!"

My head spun to hear Granny carrying on so. She headed for her broom, so I ran outside the cabin with my cousin in my arms.

Eliza's belly growled. Though Aunt Charity still nursed her in secret from time to time, the milk was ending. If only I could just go up to the big house.

Behind me, I heard the rustle of my aunt's skirts, dragging slow, half asleep. She had come home last night when the moon was high up. She flopped down beside me and cried, soft at first then louder. She wouldn't tell me what was wrong. I lay awake for a long while after she fell asleep.

I remembered the sheds in the woods behind the breeding cabins. I'd seen field hands slip inside some nights when I was up late helping Granny. Mostly they were tall men, handsome and muscled. Sometimes Master showed up too. Breeders would walk slowly down the path to the sheds, heads down, looking back like they'd forgotten something. But soon enough, they reached the sheds and went in. Maybe that's the place she had come from.

Now my aunt reached out and pushed me toward the orchard.

"Go on up, son, and let her see you and Eliza. You don't have to say nothin'. If she's got a heart, she'll know what you're askin'."

I raced through my chores that day. It was late afternoon when I ran all the way to the big house with Eliza on my shoulders, across the flat mile of orchard. By the yard, I hid behind some oaks and peeked out. Straight ahead was the big house. Master's house shone so white in the sun, it hurt my eyes. On the wraparound porch, a table was set for a tea party: strawberries ripe and red, a tray full of icing cake, milk in pitchers, cool and white. Four slaves in aprons fussed around it all. Windows were everywhere, with shiny glass looking out at me.

I signaled the nanny with birdcalls, whistling through my palms a dancing tune. Miss Layotte looked up. She was such a tiny slave, delicate, maybe twelve years old. Her waist was about as wide as my two hands. A kerchief hid her hair. But she was starched and stiff as Granny said. She marched behind the oak trees, glancing over her shoulder at the white girls playing under the apple tree in the backyard. As she walked, her hips swayed back and forth.

"Boy," Miss Layotte shook her finger at me, "what do you want? You know you're not supposed to be seen around the big house!"

"I know but . . ."

Though I was a full foot taller than Miss Layotte, I felt about as tall as a toad beside her, and as smelly as one too. I stepped back some. Maybe Granny was right. This girl wasn't black like me. Her skin shone like fine, brown wood, as if she polished it each morning. From the folds of her dress, I caught the scent of faraway roses.

"You Miss Layotte, the nanny?"

All I could do was stare at her. Almond-shaped eyes she had, deep and brown.

"What if I am?" she snapped back. "Who might you be?"

"Abram, miss. Breedin' cabin boy. I help Granny with the birthin's." I turned Eliza around in my arms. "This is my cousin."

"You take care of her all by yourself?"

She stretched herself up tall on her tippy toes, trying to stare down at us. Her boots stuck out beneath her skirts, chestnut and tiny.

"Have to, Miss Layotte. Her momma's busy cookin', and Granny's fussin' with breeders. Least she's got family, not like some."

Miss Layotte brought her head down a bit when I said that. Her long eyelashes brushed her cheeks for a good long minute like she was remembering something. Then she leaned close to study Eliza from head to toe.

I held my breath. Perhaps she'd guess the truth of it right off — that Master was her father. That creamy skin of hers was paler than ours. Her brown hair was wavy, not tight like mine. Her bright blue eyes didn't ever go away like they were supposed to.

"This baby's a beauty," the nanny admired. "Like a promise. Looks as sweet inside as she is outside."

My mouth dropped open. That's how I felt about my cousin. Miss Layotte tickled Eliza's cheek and didn't notice me anymore. Eliza smiled up at her in that way she had of wrapping you around her finger. That child reached out her arms to Miss Layotte. The next thing I knew, Miss Layotte folded Eliza into her arms. I let it be awhile, but finally I gave her a hint. I couldn't just say nothing like Aunt Charity said to do.

"It's the end of her nursin' time," I suggested. "See those fat legs of hers? And those cheeks full as a squirrel hidin' nuts? Won't be like that for long. She'll be eatin' from the troughs soon."

Miss Layotte looked over her shoulder at the white girls playing. I could see a bun at the back of her head, stretched tight and held in with a shiny pin, and her long smooth neck. She stared at the big house a long minute then turned her back to it. Quickly she reached into her apron pocket and pulled out a link of sausage. She pressed it into my hand.

"You come at dusk each night, boy." Miss Layotte set Eliza down. "I'll do what I can for this child."

No sooner had I hidden the meat in my pocket then we heard the rustle of petticoats close by.

"Why, Miss Emma and Miss Abigail," fussed Miss Layotte with a frown, "you're not supposed to follow me around!"

The youngest sister hung back some, fingers in her mouth, listening to the nanny. She was plump and so pale I could almost see through her skin like she was a moonchild. She was born around the same time as Eliza. But the oldest sister paid no mind to Miss Layotte. She spied Eliza kicking up dirt and ran right over. Her hair was spun into ringlets shining like ripe wheat in the sun. Miss Abigail was seven years to my eight years, but she was mistress over me.

Miss Abigail stared hard at Eliza's blue eyes. It made me worry until the white miss pulled up Eliza's hands and played patticake with her. Eliza was all thumbs, beating at the air instead of on Miss Abigail's hands. Eliza watched for the white hands and swatted at 'em like they were flies, but she kept missing. Miss Layotte and I smiled, thinking how Master's daughters had a new girlfriend.

Smack! We all heard Eliza's hands meeting with Miss Abigail's.

It was getting near dinnertime. I didn't want to be caught by the Master's house. I picked Eliza up. She didn't come easy though. She kicked her feet into my belly and tugged on the younger girl's dress. Miss Emma wrapped her arms around my cousin and wouldn't let go.

"Bring her back, boy!" Miss Abigail ordered me.

"Honey," Miss Layotte sweettalked her, "the boy will be bringin' her back long as you settle down now. And no talkin' about the baby to your papa. Promise me."

I yanked my cousin away from the girls and stepped back, holding her tight.

Miss Abigail set both hands on her hips and faced me straight.

"You promise to bring her back, and I'll be quiet!"

"I'll bring her back, Miss Abigail."

"You tell me when first, boy."

She was tapping her pointy white shoes on the ground, reminding me some of Granny. She was the boss for sure.

"Tomorrow evening, Miss Abigail." I sighed. "At sunset."

"Best you come every night. Then I'll keep a secret."

37

Miss Abigail grabbed her sister's hand, and they skipped back to the big house, their golden ringlets bouncing along with them. From a distance, Miss Emma smiled back at us. Miss Layotte followed behind, her skirts rustling in the night breeze like laundry waving on the line. She had her eyes on the two white girls up ahead and didn't turn back to look at us.

I ran all the way back to our cabin. It was just four pine walls with a hard packed dirt floor, but when Aunt Charity was around, she filled the place up. She was a big woman, yet she moved light on her feet, tiptoeing around the cabin like she had wings instead of feet.

I heard her sing clear and bright across the quarters.

> *I turn my eyes to-ward the sky.*
> *Ask the Lord for wings to fly.*
> *If you get there be-fore I do,*
> *look out for me.*
> *I'm com-in' too!*

By the time I had burst inside the cabin, Aunt Charity had swept the dirt floor flat and was laying the burlap down, smoothing it out for us just like a real bed. Good thing Granny wasn't around. She would have said to share the sausage with all the young 'uns.

"Miss Layotte's got a heart just like you said." I held out the sausage to my aunt.

"Take a bite, son. Give the rest to Eliza. You so busy workin' and worryin', never think about yourself."

My aunt kept fussing, complaining about how I'm so skinny, she could see all my ribs and each backbone too.

"I don't need nothin'!" I folded my arms across my chest.

It was true. Eliza was my baby just as much as she was Aunt Charity's. We were both taking a hand in raising her. Eliza's the one who'd be left after both of us were gone, like some shiny coin bringing us all good luck.

I fed Eliza all the meat.

Chapter 4

H-o-o Ah Hoo!

By the time Eliza was five, she was plump and never quiet for one moment. She worked around the breeding cabins with me. One August morning, I stood by the trough stirring up cornmeal with boiled water. I was sweating a river down my back and flinging flies away. Six babies were plopped on the ground, some barebottomed, some in burlap diapers. All of 'em watched Eliza.

"Sit still, Willie," she coaxed. "You get ready next, Annie Mae."

She was grooming those young 'uns, running her fingers through their hair like a real comb, teasing out tangles and bits of hay that got caught there. She plucked out the biting bugs. Not one of those babies shed a tear.

Breeders' babies were tended close by the

breeding cabins in the daytime. We kept an eye on 'em between cooking and cleaning. That way, their mommas could pass by and nurse 'em from time to time. Once they were five, they had a job to do every day. Some would grow up with us. Some might be sold anytime by the Master. Best not to give him an excuse, Granny would warn 'em, best to keep busy. Come night, the young 'uns slept with their mommas in the breeding cabins, but some breeders had their own cabins here and there in the quarters like us.

All around the yard, breeders were busy. I waved good morning to two field hands heavy with child, due next month. They boiled up indigo in a pot to dye homespun cloth deep blue. I couldn't help but admire that color. The women smiled as they worked, for they weren't going to bake in the sun for a time. But Granny told me they got to bring their babies home. Master mostly kept field-slave families together. He even married 'em when they asked.

"Mix it up good, Abram." Granny leaned on her cane beside me. "I'll slice some bacon fat into it next. Gonna make it so thick, that stick won't move."

I didn't tell Granny how I had seen her pour milk into the trough that mornin', stolen from Master's butter churn. It set my mouth to watering. I'd been up since dawn, washing sheets in the mile-back stream and cooking breakfast for the breeding women. I seemed tied to Granny's side. She couldn't work like she used to. Though she rubbed her back and knees each night with a hot pepper remedy, she ached deep in her bones. Nothing could straighten her up. She bent to the ground like a willow stick.

"Keep stirrin', boy, and I'll tell you about evil spirits."

"What's that?" Eliza looked up.

"Devils," whispered Granny. "Come night, they ride by on their pitchforks. If you're sleepin' deep, you might never know they come by 'cept they leave a mark on you."

Eliza gasped, but Granny leaned close and squinted at me.

"You ever see someone wake up with lines on their face, straight up-and-down lines, like something long's been scratchin' it?"

"Why Aunt Charity's got those creases up and down her face every morning!"

"That's the devil's pitchfork scrapin' her face all night. They jump on top your chest and ride you all over hell. You lyin' there asleep and can't do nothin'."

"Why do they do that?" Eliza's eyes popped out of her face.

"They need somethin' alive to ride on. Fresh blood. You ever hear someone snorin' in their sleep?"

"Why Granny, you snore most every night!" I told her.

Eliza's eyes sparkled with mischief.

"Never you mind!" I ducked my head just in time so that Granny's cane missed me. "Folks snore cause they're fightin' those spirits all night. Only one way to trap 'em."

Sharp pine needles. Some mornings I stepped on 'em with my bare feet.

"Before I go to sleep, I sprinkle pine needles around my sack. When those devils leave at sunup, they have to tiptoe over 'em to get out. Burns their feet like fire."

Granny was busy nodding her head, pleased she'd outwitted those evil spirits, when suddenly Eliza pointed. From across the orchard, dust had stirred up from the ground.

"Here comes Satan himself!" muttered Granny. "Smoke in his trail."

It was the Master riding his chestnut horse. He liked to survey his property or maybe ask Granny who had birthed a baby during the night. Sometimes, if Granny had delivered more than one boy that month, he threw a silver dollar down at her feet.

Master rode straight up to us. His blue

eyes shone from beneath his wide linen hat. He wore a white suit without a spot on it. Even his boots looked like someone spit on em and rubbed 'em to a shine.

"Granny," he called down to her from his saddle. "You keep those babies so clean, they ought to win a prize at the county fair!"

"Think I got time to fuss with babies," grumbled Granny, "when I got to boss all those breedin' women and cook dinner for the field slaves besides? Eliza's watchin' 'em, not me!"

Master turned his head toward Eliza.

"You trainin' her to do it, Granny?"

"No, sir. She does it by herself. Don't need much trainin', that one."

"How old is the child now?" he asked.

"Past five years," answered Granny.

"You, girl," his voice boomed, "what's your job?"

Eliza looked up at him and studied his blue eyes so long I trembled. Master was asking Eliza a question, and I wondered if she knew she had to speak up.

"Mindin' the babies, sir." Eliza smiled easy. "They always dirty. Always hungry. Granny and me all day busy with 'em."

The Master threw back his head and laughed.

"They gettin' smarter each day and not

scared of me either. Granny, you ought to be proud of this girl. She's a natural born worker. Train her for breedin' cabin girl."

Granny just glared at the Master like she'd have liked to throw him into the trough. Then his eyes caught mine.

"Get out from behind Granny's skirts!" Master thundered. "Let me have a look at you, boy!"

I ran up to him, shaking like a leaf from head to toe, almost tripping into the dirt at his feet. I hung my head down like I'd been taught. He looked me up and down: my flat, bare chest, bony knees, toes poking out of the beat-down shoes they gave me. Just a bone of a boy.

"You must be near eleven, boy. Old enough to leave the breedin' women. Slaves are born to pick cotton, and you are one of 'em. Tomorrow mornin', be in the fields before sunup!"

With a twist of his horse's mane, he rode off. All that was left was dust and me leaning on the pole, standing still now, no longer turning.

"See those lines on his face?" hissed Granny. "Devils been ridin' him all night. That's why he's sent you to the fields. Most days, he don't even see you. Should have crouched down, boy, and hid."

Tears sprang to my eyes. I bit my lip hard so they would not fall.

"Granny, why didn't you fight for me? You always outsmart Master."

Granny blew out a sigh loud as the north wind.

"I know what I can fight for, boy, and what I can't. One thing's sure on this plantation. Cotton's gotta be picked when it's poppin' off the branch like it is now. You gonna have to go, boy."

My job was done at the trough. I stomped off, digging my fists into my pockets. I ignored Eliza calling after me and hung my head down all the way back to the cabin.

Aunt Charity looked up breathless from sweeping the yard. Her belly stretched tight against her calico dress and her feet swelled up. She was with child again.

"What's ailin' you?" she asked in her sing-song voice.

"Master is sendin' me to the fields tomorrow mornin."

"Abram," she ran her big hand through my curls, "pick like the Master says. Work hard and the day will pass by. Come home to us at night. We'll be waitin'."

"But I don't want to go!" I pouted.

"Gettin' to be a man." Aunt Charity lifted my chin up. "Shootin' up to the sky. You're

46

ready for the fields. Only breedin' women and old men stay behind in the quarters."

I shut my eyes and laid down inside the cabin. But all I saw was the Master standing tall over me, red lines up and down his face. The conker shell blew loud three times for dinnertime. Eliza peeked into the doorway, hiding her hands behind her back.

"It's not dark yet," she pleaded. "We could still go up to the big house. Miss Abigail's gonna teach me all about tea parties."

We'd been running to Miss Layotte most every night. But I was near tears tonight. I felt older than Granny.

"I can't go tonight." I sighed.

"If you won't go now," she called from the doorway, "can we go another night when you're feelin' better, Abram?"

" 'Course we can. Those girls will wait for you."

"I brought you something." Eliza stepped inside.

She set a gourd shell in front of me, full of steaming cornmeal with bits of smoked bacon. White swirls of milk were running through it too, creamy sweet. I set the gourd against my mouth, and gulped my dinner down in one swallow.

From the quarters, I heard drumbeats throb. Somewhere field workers sat in a circle tapping on tree stumps. I always ran out soon as I heard 'em. I'd bang along on Granny's pot. But I didn't budge from my sack that night.

I could not sleep. I tossed and turned on the burlap sack, listening to Granny snore. I wanted to scream out, "I won't go!", but the words were trapped inside my bone-dry throat. All night long, I heard that chant coming closer, growing louder, beating against my door like a heartbeat, until I squeezed both fists over my ears.

"H-o-o ah hoo!" they sang to me. "H-o-o ah hoo!"

Ghost calls.

Chapter 5

Snatchin' and A-crammin' It in My Sack

Round dawn the next morning, Aunt Charity shook me awake.

"H-o-o ah hoo!" The chant was deep and low. "H-o-o ah hoo!"

It called outside my very door again and again until I rose from my sack. White vapors hung in the air thick as clouds. The old man stood there, lean and twisted as a rope. He was so skinny, I could count the bones in his face like he was a skeleton. His eyes burned through me like fire. He nodded his head at me and looked to the next cabin.

My aunt set a straw hat on my head as a good-bye. I joined the line that wound through the quarters. Workers stumbled out of their doorways. All of 'em rubbed their eyes, stretching their backs like me. They called together, a chorus of voices answering the leader's chant in the fog.

"H-o-o ah hoo!"

We headed across the cotton fields, past the rows in bloom, two miles away. As we walked, the pace picked up.

"H-o-o ah hoo!" called the leader. "H-o-o ah hoo!"

"H-o-o ah hoo! H-o-o ah hoo!" echoed the workers again and again.

We marched barefoot, stepping in time with one another. By the time we reached the fields where the overseer waited, the fog almost lifted. I was full awake. The leader leaned his head back and screamed out bold as a crow, "H-o-o a-h-h-h h-o-o-o-o!"

It no longer seemed like a chant or even sorrow, but just as if he was telling me, "I brought you here. Brought you because it was my job. But I'll stay beside you. I will not leave you alone."

All was quiet again. I looked out across the fields and gasped. It was a field of white. You couldn't count the bushes if you had all day. Some cotton was in boll, some in flower. Light shone from that cotton like the sun. I remembered Granny telling me how once she saw snow, and it must have been like this. Clean and bright as if the earth was just born.

But I couldn't admire too long. That overseer poked his stick into my back and pushed me down a row so hard I nearly fell over.

"Get crackin' boy!" he yelled as he tossed me a bag. "Strap this sack around your shoulders and fill it."

I grabbed a boll of cotton sitting there like a cloud, but it didn't feel like a cloud. It bit me right away. My fingers got caught in a dry shell that snapped like a mousetrap. That cotton didn't slip out easy. All around me, hands shot out like lightning bugs, two hands at a time, one grabbing to the left, the other to the right. Each traveled back to the sack with a fistful of cotton. But when I grabbed the cotton, it bounced away from me. *Crack!* A branch snapped in two.

Getting the cotton in my sack was another thing. Most folks just tossed it in, not even looking where it was headed. Sacks were bulging full in no time. I threw it in mine, but my sack didn't fill up as I moved down the row. Behind me, cotton bolls had dropped onto the ground, all brown. I rubbed 'em against my shirt then popped 'em into my sack.

I had started with a partner on the other side of me, but he was long gone, bushes ahead of me. Once or twice, he had whispered, "Keep your hand steady. Reach into the bushes easy, boy." I must have been shaking them up like a mighty storm.

Then I felt the stick poking into my backbone.

"Breakin' all the branches, boy!" the overseer yelled. "No buds gonna bloom on a broken branch."

That stick pressed so deep I could hardly breathe.

"Take a step to your right. Pick!"

I could always wiggle away from Granny's broom, but I couldn't budge from that stick of his. Sweat poured down my back. My hands reached out stiffly. I tugged a boll and aimed it in my sack with both hands. I reached out again and my elbow bent into another branch. *Snap!* It cracked. A bud dropped to my feet, and I watched it go down with a gasp.

I heard the zing of wind first then felt the three slaps of his hickory whip against my bare back. I had never been whipped before, but I'd been told what to do. Stand still. Don't flinch. Don't fall over. But the whip burned, stinging hot, flashing pain all through me.

Next thing I knew, the overseer was so close to me, I saw the week's worth of beard stubble on his bloated red face. His belly hung loose above his belt. I could even hear his breath, seesawing heavy, like he was working hard.

"You just a boy, so you lucky," he sneered at me. "Twenty-five lashes for men who break a bud. Keep your mind on the cotton!"

I looked dead ahead at the cotton, its cloud whiteness all I could see. I tried not to think how my whipburn glowed. I dragged myself from row to row. The sun burned my neck like fire. Seemed I picked for hours. After a while, the overseer moved on down the row.

What was Eliza doing without me? I wondered. I didn't want to leave her behind, but I didn't want to take her here either. It didn't matter what I wanted anyhow. I forgot about the workers around me until from across the field rose the call, "Woh hoo-oo! Woh ho!"

Then from my right, came an answering call, "Yeh-ee-eh!"

Here and there, calls rose up like partridges fluttering out of the bushes where you didn't expect them to. Then the calls died down. Every once in a while, they started up again. I lifted my head to see who was calling, but no one was in sight. Once I yelled out in that field of white that stretched forever far, "Woh hoo-oo!"

After a long minute an answer echoed, "Yeh-ee-eh!"

When the sun hung over my head and didn't move but just glowed like a golden ball, the overseer blew a conker shell five times. Noon. Women flew, feet leaping behind them like deer hooves, headed for the shade of the oak trees. Betty, a nursing breeder, stumbled across the field, a pail in her hand and a sack dragging over her shoulder.

"Careful, Abram," she fussed when I grabbed her pail. "I already spilled half of it. Won't be no water left to drink."

Beneath the oak tree, mothers nursed their babies. They'd been crawling over the ground alone all morning, covered with dust, streaks of tears running down their faces. Now they were rocking quiet in their mothers' laps. A few toddlers ran up to Betty and yanked at her skirts, reaching up for a cornpone from her sack. They dropped their heads back and opened their mouths wide for the few drops of water I poured down their throats. Then off they ran to their mommas.

Workers swallowed cornpones like they were just air. Each one dipped the gourd in the bucket for one long sip then passed it around to the next one. Soon the men stretched out on the ground. There were a hundred of us in all. The women wore potato-sack dresses with calico cloths on their heads, young and old. Men were barechested, with suspenders holding up their pants. Most were barefooted all summer long. The faces of old slaves were creased like dry leather. But their skin sparkled in the sun: the coal black of Ben's string-bean arms, the coffee brown of my partner's face, and the burnt copper of some who had Cherokee blood.

I watched Betty stumble back across the hazy field, hand over her forehead to block the sun. The babies yawned, full of milk.

"Rest up now," the old man whispered in my ear. "Later on, we'll pick it up. Grab some time before he comes by. I'll wake you."

I lay on my side so that I wouldn't touch my sore back to the ground. I closed my eyes and drifted, but all I saw was cotton bolls big as clouds. Even resting, I couldn't stop picking 'em. Someone shook me awake. I stumbled to my feet. The sun had moved an inch across the sky. We headed back to the rows. Behind us, babies slept in a heap.

The old man sang to us.

Come a-cross child-ren. Don't get lost.
Spread your rod and come a-cross!

He paced up and down the rows. His voice trailed from far off like wind. I stood straight up and picked up speed.

The field workers answered.

We have come a-cross!

Slaves stood in full sun, their bare backs shiny with sweat. Muscles popped up everywhere, from their chests down to their fingertips. Beside them, I was a brown twig.

The leader reminded us.

Don't get lost!
Spread your rod and come a-cross.

After a while, the voices died out. The hours moved slow. The sun stood still in the sky, drilling heat so deep, it heated up my bones. My arms were two deadweights. Fingers scratched against dry bolls. Bushes rustled in the wind. Silence.

I looked up. My partner looked up. We turned our heads like owls in all directions. North. South. East. West. We scanned our eyes low to the cotton bushes up and down the endless rows. Overseer had gone for a nap under the oaks. That's when I heard the humming, like notes buzzing from the throat of a bee. Bass notes. High notes. The workers hummed in tune with one another, trying to find the right note.

The leader yelled to us.

> *Would-n't drive so hard but . . .*
> *I need your arms!*
> *Would-n't drive so hard but . . .*
> *I need your arms!*"

The pickers answered.

> *Snatch-in' and a-cram-min'*
>   *it in my sack.*
> *Got-ta have some cot-ton*
>   *if it breaks my back.*

The leader called again.

> *Would-n't drive so hard but*
> *I need your arms!*
> *Would-n't drive so hard but*
> *I need your arms!*

My jaw hung open like a door. I stood stock still, listening. I knew I should be picking, but I heard something, the sound the words made as the workers sang out. There was such a beat, I wanted to tap my bare feet against the ground and shake my body across the row. But I couldn't do that. I was scared of that whip finding me.

I did the one thing that wouldn't get me in trouble. I shook my head up and down, up when they began a word, and down when they ended. I reached out for the cotton in between. I moved down that row double-time. My sack filled fast now.

> *Would-n't drive so hard but . . .*
> *I need your arms!*

The old man stood on the other side of the row. He crowed so loud it was impossible not to hear him and impossible not to do what he asked. I never dreamed my dead, heavy arms could pick so fast. He picked up the beat, shouting and beating his palms against his thighs. Only then did I notice the old man wasn't picking. He was driving us to pick.

Hours later, the conker shell blasted. Three times. It was dusk. The sun melted down into the edge of the field, red as blood. Though I was drenched in sweat and my arms drooped, heavy as logs, I raised my fists to the sky and shouted, "Done! Done! Done!"

The old man grinned at me, his lined face stretched tight as drumskin. I fell in line behind him. We were a long rope of slaves, winding back to the quarters.

"H-o-o ah hoo!" he sighed at us. "H-o-o ah hoo!"

"H-o-o ah hoo! H-o-o ah hoo!" we echoed his call.

One by one, we were dropped off at our cabin doors. The old man turned back and waved me off, still singing. The face that looked like it was carved in rock shone back in the darkness at me.

I dragged myself through the door. Aunt Charity came over to me right away. She turned my hands over in hers and saw the blisters. I heard her gasp when I turned around. She led me to the burlap and patted my whipburn with cool grease. Then she smoothed down my hands so they felt like baby skin.

"You know they sing out there?" I finally said. "All day long."

"Ben makes the work go easy," she answered.

Eliza popped open one eye. She was all curled up on the burlap. She smiled with her eyes half shut, yawning. I hugged her good night. She was limp in my arms.

"Ben sings in the mornings when we're sad!" I rocked Eliza back to sleep. "Chants in the afternoons when we drop like dead flies. Yanks us up like puppets on a string to pick a storm."

"Gets inside you, that man's singin'," Granny piped up from her corner. "He puts a feelin' into all his words."

My aunt and Granny talked 'til deep dark. My body plopped down to the ground like a sack. I couldn't sit up anymore. I tucked Eliza into the burlap between Aunt Charity and me, her dark hair spread across us both like black wings.

My eyes shut tight. I was gonna call out to Granny that I didn't care if the devils rode by that night, 'cause if they did, I wouldn't even feel it. But I couldn't talk anymore.

Just wanted sleep, sweet sleep, for now.

Chapter 6

In My Lady's Chamber

I carried my sack beneath that Alabama sun for the next two years, fingers blistering and never healing, bent over the cotton bushes, a deep sore that never let up biting into my back. I did as Aunt Charity said. I did what I had to all day long just so Master would let me be. It was dusk when I tramped home from the fields, thirsting deep. I headed straight to the breeding cabins to look for Eliza.

Sometimes I'd find her hugging those babies like she was their momma though she was only seven. Other times she'd be carting buckets from the stream for the birthings. But this one time, Eliza squatted by the trough, stirring pork fat into corn grits with a long stick. Beside her, Chloe's son poured water into the grits like Granny taught us, to make it look like there was more food. Eliza lifted her hand to swat a fly and spied me. Quick as lightning flashing, that girl was up running. Hair flying and long legs jumping in the air, Eliza somersaulted into my arms, head upside down, giggling up a storm.

"Squawk! Squawk!" she screamed. "What do the crows say today?"

"They say Eliza's tummy is grumblin' for some real food!" I screeched back at her.

"C'mon, Abram, let's go for a ride!" she crowed. "Up to the big house to see what's there."

We'd been stopping there whenever I had time. But it was high cotton season. It'd been weeks since we'd gone. So I scooped up a fistful of grits and slid it down my bone-dry throat. With Eliza cawing and kicking up a racket in my arms like some crow, I forgot all about my aching back. I set her on top my shoulders and ran across the orchard, telling stories as I went.

They were stories about how the crows buzzed each morning when I walked to the fields, lifting off the cotton bushes to spread their wings across the sky. How, some days, they complained it's gonna be real hot. Other days, they were just plain mad and screamed at each other for hours. Sometimes they tumbled all upside down in the sky before a storm blew in, or maybe they'd gather together, all the crows in the county, when something bad was gonna happen. You never knew what they were gonna squawk next.

"Crows sure are lucky." Eliza's voice in my ear was full of wonder. "Get to ride the wind as it blows in. Don't have to wait for it to come by like us."

I twirled my arms around like wild wind, spinning Eliza in circles.

"Caw! Caw!" she screeched all the way to the big house.

We didn't have time to hide behind the oak tree. Miss Layotte stood in the yard, hands on her hips, looking our way. Miss Emma spied us coming and started running. Her sister waved up a mighty storm, but Miss Layotte ordered them both to stay behind in the yard. She stepped towards us, her mouth set in one flat line.

"Where you been these past weeks, boy? My girls a-waitin' on Eliza. I had a mighty time holdin' them back from tellin' their father!"

"High cotton season, Miss Layotte. By the time I come home, it's near dark. Soon as I eat dinner, I fall asleep."

Miss Layotte eyed me up and down like I had turned into a green toad. She leaned close to my ear to whisper, "You don't care if Eliza misses some extra food?"

" 'Course I do! She needs it for growin'."

"Food gone to waste, boy," she hissed at me. "Fed it to the birds!"

I hung my head down and wouldn't let her see my scowling face. Here Eliza had gone to bed hungry all week, and this nanny just threw good food away.

"You promise to come here every night, boy," she tapped her finger on my chest, "and I'll save something for Eliza."

I gritted my teeth tight together.

"I promise, miss."

Soon as I said it, I wanted to slam my foot against the ground. It was a promise I couldn't keep. I'd be back by fall the earliest. Why does everyone make me promise something? I'd made a heap of promises to Eliza. Granny too. I'd promised Miss Emma and Miss Abigail to bring Eliza by. And now I had to promise this nanny too! She bossed me around though she was just a slave herself.

Next thing I knew, Eliza jumped down from my arms like a cat. Before I could stop her, she skipped right up to the nanny.

"You so pretty, miss. Smell like flowers." She slipped her hand into the nanny's. "Granny says you sleep in a real bed. Is it true?"

I watched Miss Layotte. House slaves put on airs, like Granny said, but she looked warm under her starched collar though the night air was cool.

"Why, child, it's just a straw mat set on the floor. Never can tell when Miss Abigail will call me. Come mornin', I roll it up."

"It's not the ground like Abram and me got."

Miss Layotte didn't know which way to look, at Eliza or me, so she looked at the white girls instead. Miss Abigail was pointing her finger straight in her little sister's face. Miss Emma just nodded her head and looked up at her with wide blue eyes.

"I bet you get to take a bath!" Eliza crowed, touching the smooth inside of the nanny's arm.

"Why, Master and Missus make me, child," confessed the nanny. "Say slaves stink same as animals. Won't let me stay inside unless I wash with soap every day."

"Soap?" gasped Eliza. "Is that what I smell? It's like roses!"

Eliza pressed her nose to the nanny's arm and sighed. Then just like that, she bolted off to the backyard where the two sisters were calling after her. She joined her hands with Miss Emma's hands to make a circle. Miss Abigail stood in the middle of the girls,

dodging in and out beneath their arms as
Eliza sang.

Ran-sum scan-sum, through yon-der.
Bring me a gourd to drink wat-er.
This way out and the oth-er way in,
in my la-dy's chamber.

I caught the hint of a smile on the nanny's
face so that I dared whisper, "Is it true what
Granny says, about you being Creole and
comin' from far away?"

Miss Layotte tossed her head toward the
big house and straightened her shoulders.

"Master paid a high price for a Creole
nanny. Brags about me to all his guests. Just
like you have to pick a heap of cotton, I must
be the best nanny there ever was!"

I got a chance to study her face, how her
eyelashes brushed her cheeks, how she kept
them down for long minutes. When she
looked up, her eyes were darker than I remembered and dewy too. She brushed her
eyes dry and marched right across the yard.
I followed close behind her swirling skirts.

The two sisters sat at a table in fluffy
dresses all pink and lacey, like wrapped-up
birthday presents I'd spied once while
hiding in the yard when Miss Abigail had a
party. Set on the table were pieces of ginger

cake, iced tea, and napkins. Eliza must have studied the serving maids on the porch before. She curtsied and held out the hem of her burlap sack like it was a uniform. She poured tea into tall glasses without spilling one drop.

"Would you like some cake with your tea, Miss Abigail?"

"I would," Miss Abigail pointed, "and a napkin for my lap too."

"Miss Emma, what can I serve you?"

"Give my sister two pieces of cake right now!" Miss Abigail bossed. "Mama always says to be a lady and take just one, but she can eat them both right now!"

Miss Emma ate her ginger cake with tiny bites that took forever. She set the second piece back onto the table, patting her full belly. Her sister pushed it back onto her plate.

"Eat it!" she ordered. "Momma will never let you eat so much. We always have to behave like ladies in front of her."

Those girls chewed for the longest time. Eliza followed every bite of that cake with her eyes as it went from the plate into their mouths. She watched as they licked the last crumb off their forks. Miss Abigail tapped her fork loudly on the table. Eliza jerked.

"More . . . tea, Miss Abigail?"

"Yes, maid. And I'll take another slice of cake too."

Eliza swallowed hard. It was the last slice of cake, and I knew she was hoping for a bite. She leaned toward it. I cleared my throat loudly. Eliza scooped up the cake and set it flat on her mistress's plate.

My blood was boiling. I stepped toward my cousin. It was time to go home. But then a scent of roses sprang up all around me like I was standing in a flower bed. Miss Layotte whispered in my ear. "Just wait, boy! I saved something special for Eliza."

Miss Layotte fussed around the table like a whirlwind, gathering all the tea things back onto the tray.

"Time to go inside, Miss Abigail and Miss Emma. You've had a lovely tea party. Dark is falling down, and your momma will be a-waitin' for you inside."

Then she smiled at my cousin.

"Child, you learn quick. Serve tea just as good as our own maids. Isn't that right, Miss Abigail?"

"If Eliza cared to brush me off so I look like a lady," she announced, "maybe I'll say she's as good as our own maids."

Eliza sprung forward so fast I thought she'd trip into Miss Abigail's lap. She brushed crumbs off the white girl's dress and set her ringlets back on her shoulder. Miss Abigail lifted her chin high and never once looked at Eliza, just sat in her chair scowling.

"Thank you for the tea party," smiled Miss Emma.

"Eliza, I understand your cousin may be busy from now on." Miss Abigail stood up. "My papa says the cotton's coming in fast. But I expect you here every night even if Abram can't come."

"I promise," answered Eliza quietly.

Miss Abigail bounced off to the house lively as could be, yanking her sister with her. Miss Emma waved goodbye until we couldn't see her anymore. I would have cussed, but I jammed my mouth shut instead. It's best if you don't speak when you're boiling up. I headed toward the oak tree. Eliza trailed right behind me.

"Miss Abigail's so fine in her long dresses and curled up hair. I wish I could be like her."

"You don't want to be like her!" I yelled. "Bosses her own sister. Doesn't listen to her nanny."

"She does what she wants though. Says what she wishes. We can't do that."

"She's the boss, that one."

"What makes her a boss instead of a slave?"

"She's Master's daughter," I spat. "White, not black like me."

Eliza held her bare arm next to mine.

"Why do I look like I'm in the middle? Not as dark as you. Or as light as them. A different color altogether. What does that make me?"

My heart did not pump for a full minute.

"Makes you Eliza," I blurted out, "my cousin."

"But does it make me a slave?"

"You born to Aunt Charity," I explained. "She's a slave. Any child of hers is a slave too. No matter what the color."

Footsteps rushed behind me. Petticoats rustled and then stopped.

"You forgot what I promised, boy."

Miss Layotte stood breathless behind us. She turned in all directions. Bright lights shone from every window in the big house, but we stood in night shadow. She reached up into the boughs of the tree and pulled down a package. Inside were two honey sandwiches.

"Eat this, child." She handed one to Eliza. "You waited long enough."

Eliza didn't gulp it down like I would have. She skipped back to the table and sat right down in a chair, spreading her burlap sack like a pretend dress. She pulled a napkin from the tray and spread it across her lap. She bit into her sandwich with tiny bites, leaning her head back like Miss Abigail.

I roared aloud, my laughter shooting straight up to the stars.

"Close your eyes," Miss Layotte ordered me. "Open your mouth and bite!"

It was soft, melting soft at first. The liquid was sweet and warm as sunshine pouring down my throat.

"Mmm!" I murmured. "Honey!"

A rose cloud drifted around me. When I opened my eyes, Miss Layotte stood so close, her stiff collar poked into my shoulder. Her worried almond eyes studied my face. That nanny looked so serious about a sandwich, I threw my head back and hooted like an owl. Miss Layotte giggled, her fine long fingers pressed over her mouth.

"You ever tasted honey before, Abram?"

It was the first time she called me Abram, and it melted down inside me just as sweet as that honey.

"Once I stole honey from a hive, but those bees chased after me and stung me up good, so I never did get to taste it. Sure is sweet!"

Eliza was already skipping away and tugging at my hand to go home. I let her pull me along.

But I heard Miss Layotte cry out in the dark, "Will you come back tomorrow?"

"We'll come!" Eliza called back to her.

"Promise me!"

"I promise, Miss Layotte!" I shouted, hoping it'd come true.

We hummed home across that orchard, Eliza and me, like we both had sprouted bird wings.

Chapter 7

Hush-a-by!
Don't You Cry

It was winter when Aunt Charity was ready to deliver her last child. All her babies had disappeared from the plantation. Four babies had come and gone overnight, and I never got to see one. I'd never crept into the breeding cabin, holding my breath, like I did on Eliza's born day. I'd never gotten the chance to say good-bye. I wasn't sure where they went or if they lived. This baby was her sixth one.

But they were my cousins same as Eliza.

My aunt had never asked me to come by the breeding cabin. Each time, she stayed overnight. Next day, she came back home, face flat and gray as a rainy day and eyes dim like a lamp burned out.

"Lost it, Abram," she sighed.

She wouldn't tell more. But the dimness

stayed there on her face. She never gave me smiles anymore.

All the long day, when I was in the fields, just fretting was all I did. There's things I knew and things I never wanted to know, but now I had to know everything. Questions burned me up like fever.

"Who is the father of this baby?" I burst into our cabin one evening and stood looking down at my aunt, resting on the floor.

"Same one who's daddy to all my babies," she whispered.

"Master?"

Aunt Charity reached for my hand, but I stepped back.

"He's no daddy to any of us," I spit the words out. "Just a boss!"

She jerked suddenly like I slapped her.

"Abram," she choked, "don't stir up trouble now!"

"Why can't I see 'em just once before they go?" I begged.

My aunt shook her head. Something brightened her eyes, and I knew they were tears.

"Please let me see this baby when it's born. Just this once!"

"I can't let you, Abram." Tears poured down her cheek. "Feel like I'm gonna lose my mind each time it happens."

My breath sucked out of me like it never was gonna come back.

"Why do you let it happen?" I stamped my foot to the floor.

My aunt pushed herself up. She stepped close enough for me to see the shiny black circles under her eyes. She grabbed me by both shoulders and shook me hard. She'd never touched me like that before.

"He ordered me to be his mistress! Don't want no one but me," she hollered. "If he tells me to jump high as the moon, I just got to do it somehow, best I can."

I watched and waited for the born day. Some nights, I'd sneak to the edge of the quarters where the workers drummed. Sometimes I just listened. Mostly I watched every flick of their fingers. Once they called me close to bang on their drums. I drummed 'til my arms ached.

Then one night, my aunt and Granny both slept overnight in the breeding cabin. Next morning, they didn't come back home. Eliza rushed into our cabin, breathless. Her eyes looked like storm clouds, dark and gray.

"Momma's got to stay in bed," she panted. "Granny says she's gonna lose the baby if she gets up. She's askin' for you to come."

She shivered from head to toe, teeth chattering in a damp corner of the cabin. I hugged her tight.

"Who's askin'?" I asked when she quieted down.

"Granny."

I shook my head, laid down, and faced the bare wall. I slept by myself in that empty cabin. But Eliza didn't leave me be. She rushed in every hour to tug at me to get up.

"Come see my momma, Abram!" she begged.

Eliza looked pale, like all the blood was drained out of her. But I shook my head again.

"Hush girl! Run on back and stay with your momma. I'll come by later."

She ran out the door, twisting her head back to see if I was coming behind her.

I didn't go. Don't know what came over me, but I didn't go.

I was walking home from the back field that evening, hoe dragging behind me, when I heard the crows. I never liked to see just one. One's bad. It gives me shivers just to think of it. You don't know what's gonna happen. All you know is it's bad. There was plenty of squawking above my head that night. I looked up and counted the crows one by one. Six crows blackened the sky.

Six is death, Granny says.

I ran to the cabin and hid my head beneath the burlap. When you're alone, you get to remembering. I thought of a winter when I was sick with the whooping cough. I must have been only four. One night I couldn't breathe. Granny thought I was fixing to die. Aunt Charity sprinkled pine-needle tea into my mouth. She stayed awake and stroked my throat that long-ago night. She smoothed down my hair that was so wet with sweat, it curled up all around my face. She laid her hands there until I fell asleep.

Mother's hands, I called them, but I'd never told her that. She had big hands to match the rest of her. I'd never told her either how, when I fell asleep that night, I dreamed I floated on a soft cloud with my momma, her face bright as moonlight. That's the place I always go when Aunt Charity runs her hands across my head, whispering as I fall asleep, "It'll be alright, Abram."

Tears poured down my face. But when I shut my eyes, I saw the crows again. Six black ones. All I could think was, this was the sixth cousin coming. Soon it would be gone.

Eliza tapped hard at the window, her face pinched tight.

I shot up from that floor.

"You sleep here, Eliza." I tucked her in the burlap sack. "You been up too many nights with your momma. My turn now."

I left Eliza there on the floor. Her eyes bulged out of her face as she stared up at the ceiling, fingers squeezed in her mouth. I piled all the burlap I could find on top of her.

The breeding cabins were set back of the row of slave quarters. It seemed I flew there in minutes. I knelt right down on the floor beside my aunt. She panted through her mouth like she couldn't get enough air. Sweating stains darkened her nightgown. The pains came, like thunder and lightning together. They broke out all over Aunt Charity, flashed quick and hard, stopped, then started up again. They came quicker and harder by the moment.

I petted her curls slow and soft and pressed cool cloths to her forehead. Sometime in the middle of the night, she squeezed my hand so hard, I felt all my bones.

Then the baby came. It was a boy child, tan-skinned like Eliza. His head was covered with Aunt Charity's curls.

Now I knew why my aunt never wanted me to come by. All of us stared through the darkness toward the big house. Granny's jaw was set square and tight, so I knew she was cursing under her breath. My Aunt Charity squeezed that baby boy like she never wanted to let him go.

I watched my newborn cousin in her arms and thought how my momma never got to hold me. At least my aunt got the chance. Maybe, just maybe, I hoped, that boy would remember someday, remember he was held and rocked all the long night through when he was born.

She sang in a whisper so that no one would even know he was born yet.

Hush-a-by! Don't you cry.
Go to sleep lit-tle ba-by.
And when you wake, you shall have a cake
and all the pret-ty lit-tle po-nies.

I closed my eyes and pretended it was my momma singing me a lullaby, a newborn baby song.

Then I sang along with my aunt.

Hush-a-by! Don't you cry.
Go to sleep lit-tle ba-by.

We never named him, just called him baby. If we had named him, he'd have been too much a part of us.

We fell asleep on the breeding cabin floor but woke at dawn to a pounding on the door. A hammering that shook the floorboards. Aunt Charity was screaming. She was in her nightgown, beating on the cabin door, nailed shut from the outside.

"Bring him back!" shrieked my aunt. "He's mine!"

Through the window we saw the overseer clutching the newborn baby in his arms like a piece of stolen meat.

"Shut up, woman!" he spit back at her. "This here child belongs to the Master. It never belonged to you!"

Before I could stop her, my aunt lifted herself out the open window and tore after him. Her nightgown was flying in the air, so maybe she didn't see it coming. She didn't hear me yell to warn her either, a step behind her. Overseer's whip flashed out and slapped her hard too many times to count. My aunt fell down to the ground. She didn't hold her hands over her head to hide either as she taught me to do. Blood spilled out from her nightgown and soaked it through and through.

The baby was gone, gone in a bundle in a white man's arms.

We carried Aunt Charity inside. I ran quick to boil up bitter herbs, while Granny greased her whipburns. She laid down for two weeks, sleeping mostly. She hardly said a word. Master came by. Spat on the floor when he saw her. Scowling mad he was.

Granny just shook her head when she tended my aunt.

"Is she gonna get better?" I begged her.

"Oh, she's gonna live alright," snapped Granny. "But she can't have babies anymore. Don't know how Master's gonna take to that."

Eliza asked a thousand questions about the baby who had come and gone overnight: if he had cried loud when he was born, if he was tan like her, and was he her brother.

The news came from Miss Layotte, whispered from mouth to ear until it came down to us. The boy child was sold at auction to a master of a far-off sugar plantation in South Carolina. If he lived, he'd work the fields there. As far away as the icy stars in a winter's sky.

Chapter 8

Come A-long
There's a Meetin'
Here Tonight

Early one dark April morning, I heard Ben call and thought surely I must be dreaming. "H-o-o ah hoo!" drummed into my ears where I lay sleeping on the floor. I stumbled to the door and grabbed the leather strips they gave me for shoes, strapped 'em on tight with ropes, and left. My aunt did not budge. Eliza slept with her arms stretched across her momma's chest. Granny curled up like a baby in a tight ball. Outside, heavy footsteps stamped across the quarters, and a hundred sighs blew like fog.

We wound like a long caterpillar heading to the fields.

The overseer was a black shadow waiting to grab us, tall and skinny with a potbelly hanging above his leather belt. He spit hard, flashing his whip like a lightning rod above our heads.

"Hoe double time this morning. Get these beds built around the plants before rain comes."

His whip snapped on the air like a live snake.

"Move, boy!" I jumped to the furrow.

It was storm season. We hoed between the heavy rains. We scraped around the new-born cotton plants and heaved weeds away, leaving only cotton behind to soak up the rain. There were fewer workers on rainy days. Mothers were allowed to stay home with their young 'uns. We'd have to pick faster without 'em. I set my feet at the end of the mile-long row. A mule far ahead of me churned up soil with a plough. In between, a hundred workers hacked soil, keeping a pace. Ben warned me not to pass anyone. You had to be careful not to follow too close or you stumbled.

"Gotta keep up," chanted in my head. "Keep your eye on the hoe and your feet straight ahead."

I tried not to think of Aunt Charity. Instead I thought of Miss Layotte and how that whiff of roses followed her like a cloud wherever she went. But I hadn't seen her lately. I stayed by my aunt most evenings. Her feet puffed up with the heat. She wasn't young anymore. I worried Master wouldn't want her. Women slaves were all worn out by the time they were twenty-five. My aunt was tired by dinnertime, so I made her lie down while I helped Granny in the breeding cabins. But I pushed Eliza out the door without me so that she could run up to the big house every night like Miss Abigail ordered.

"It's a comin'!" My partner ahead of me looked up at the black cloud riding in from the north, covering the gray ones.

Ben paced down the row, sniffing the air.

"Got an hour before it comes down. Let's beat it," he announced. "A mile-long row to hoe before he lets us go."

"How we gonna do it?" I gasped.

A length of row that long would take three hours to hoe. The black cloud was sailing in fast. Ben cleared his throat and stood tall.

"Woh hoo-oo!" he announced to the field. "Woh hoo-oooo!"

Every head turned his way along the mile-long row. His voice lifted up so loud behind me, it roared.

Get you rea-dy!
There's a meet-in' here to-night.
Come a-long!
There's a meet-in' here to-night.

Beside me workers called out.

There's a fire in the east.

The answer echoed from far off.

There's a fire in the west.

And winding through it, was Ben's voice like an invitation.

Come to the camp meet-in' in the wil-der-ness!

It was a sparkly song that lit everyone up as if we were on fire. Feet stomped down the row to the beat. Hoes scraped the dirt, busy as cricket wings chirping. Ben passed around a breakfast of cornpones. We swallowed 'em standing straight up and dared not stop hoeing. I picked up weeds just a bush behind my partner now, so we could talk sometimes.

"Gonna be a meetin' tonight," my partner whispered, his eyes bright. "Come Saturday night, always a meetin' of some sort."

"What kind of meetin' is it gonna be?"

"Last week was a prayer meetin' where most everyone, even the old folks, went." He winked. "But tonight, there's a dance where only the young ones go."

He looked at me close and asked, "How old are you boy?"

"Thirteen and then some months."

"About time for you to go to a Saturday night dance."

I'd heard about such meetings before. But Granny and my aunt never sneaked off on Saturday nights. Their work was never done is why. I had no chores that night but stayed in the quarters in case Granny needed me. Most nights are the same for slaves except for Saturday night. That one night shone like freedom 'cause the next day we didn't have to work the fields. We went to church, tended our gardens, and visited instead. Saturday night, a hush lay over the quarters, a holding-our-breath, waiting-for-Sunday kind of hush.

A deep rumble shook the ground so hard, it cracked the dry ground around the cotton bushes. In the next second, rain pelted down in pinpricks that hurt my head.

"Finish that row!" the overseer shouted at us.

All around us, dirt turned into mud. It was everywhere, flung upwards with our hoes, falling down on our heads. Our feet sunk fast into it. And that rain just kept on, soaking through my shirt. Overseer cursed and lashed his whip until we reached the end of the row.

"Come a-cross chil-dren!" shrieked Ben. "Don't get lost!"

He waved us toward the direction of the slave quarters.

"We have come across!" we screamed at him.

We sang in the rain with foolish grins, for our work day was done early. Soon we would be home. I leaned my head back and let that rain tickle my dry throat. I got a Saturday bath. For just this once, I would be as clean as Miss Layotte though I had no soap.

The yard outside the breeding cabins was empty and churned with mud. I walked on. Ben dropped me by my cabin. "Rest now. The week is done," he said.

Rest was the last thing on my mind. The door to our cabin was pushed wide open. Sprawled on the front porch were ten young 'uns, hiding from the rain. They shot clay marbles into one another's wide-open hands. I remember Eliza had dropped 'em into the dye pot and baked those marbles in the sun some days ago. I stepped across the children and burst into our cabin, where I knew Eliza would be waiting for me. She was eight now, tall and wiry. She was stretched out on the burlap, staring up at the ceiling, two babies asleep in her arms. She was listening to rain tap on the hard tin roof, its pitter-patter filling the cabin so loud I had to yell, "Girl! I'm home!"

She turned her head toward me but didn't come rushing over like she always did. She just rocked the babies slowly back and forth. I plopped down beside her, folding some burlap on the dirt beneath me so that the mud didn't soak through.

"What's ailin' you girl?"

"You remember what it was like in the breedin' cabins?" she asked, without answering me.

"Always busy you mean, with Granny bossin' besides."

"Don't mind bein' busy." She sighed. "It's the stillness I mind."

I pointed to the toddlers playing. "It's not quiet in here!"

"Granny ordered me to take 'em away from the cabins." She fixed her eyes on me. "Didn't want 'em to see . . . but I saw, Abram."

I sat straight up. Eliza stared up at the ceiling for a long while before speaking.

"Chloe's gone. Granny did all she could."

"Chloe?"

Chloe was a breeder older than Aunt Charity, prized for delivering eight babies, one each year. She had been in labor late last night when I went to bed.

"Hush!" warned Eliza, looking over at a boy throwing marbles high up and catching 'em as they fell back down. "He's Chloe's firstborn."

"What happened to her?" I whispered now.

"Her baby wouldn't come out. Granny pushed and pulled and worked spells. Chloe screamed all night long. Then she grew so still. We couldn't wake her. She died this morning."

Eliza squeezed the babies so tight in her arms, I thought they would awaken.

"Granny and you did your best." I patted her shoulder.

"Granny said Chloe birthed too many babies too fast. Her body gave out. But she didn't have a choice."

Eliza looked at me with bloodshot eyes.

"I can help the breeders, but I can't stop 'em dyin'. I can tend the babies, but I can't keep 'em from being sold."

"No one can."

"Got no choice about myself either. If Master decides someday I'll be a breeder, that's what I'll be."

My face burned same as if I'd been slapped. I remembered my own momma who was just five years older than my cousin when she birthed me.

"Someday you'll be head of the breedin'

cabins like Granny," I reminded her. "That's what she's trainin' you for."

"I don't want nothin' to do with the breedin' cabins!" she shot back at me.

The call of crows trailed into the cabin. Rain must have been breaking up somewhere. They flew past the window high in the sky, pumping their wings a long mile before they disappeared.

"Wish we be like the crows, child." Granny stuck her head in the doorway and shooed the young 'uns to come for feeding at the trough. "They are the only ones free."

Granny stumbled off, half asleep on her feet, the toddlers screaming and yanking on her skirts.

"Listen!" Eliza pointed up to the roof. The tapping was lighter now, like tears falling from trees. "What are we wastin' time for? Let's run up to the big house."

"Too early, girl. It's near lunchtime. Folks at the big house will be hidin' inside, away from the rain."

"We could just go see." She pulled me to my feet. "Maybe the girls sneaked out and got nothin' to do."

I grabbed her hand, and we raced through the orchard in and out of the peach trees. By the oaks, we crouched down. Singing drifted into our ears from the yard. At first, it sounded like humming, low humming. I tightened Eliza's hand in mine and leaned my head forward. I heard deep sobs. After a while, it stopped, and there came such a silence, I thought someone had seen us. I pressed my back flat against the tree as if I were part of it. I didn't even breathe.

But the words reached me.

> *Well, I'm drift-in' and drift-in'*
> *just like a ship out to sea.*
> *Drift-in'. Drift-in'.*

The song was sung soft and low like a lullaby, but there was no sweetness to it, only sorrow. I knew that voice. Though I had never heard her sing, I heard the way she sang it with a trace of a Creole accent. It was Miss Layotte. It was such a mournful tune, so unexpected, that I wiped my eyes dry.

> *Well I ain't got no-bo-dy in this whole world*
> *who cares for me.*
> *I'm drift-in' like a ship out to sea.*

I never imagined that nanny feeling so low. I pictured her crisp in her rustling dress, her dark eyes snapping, ordering me around. Her collar must be all wet with tears. I pressed a finger to my lips, bent low to the ground, and yanked Eliza out of there. We stopped in the middle of the orchard, trees standing around us like guards.

"What we got to hide here for?" fussed Eliza.

"Miss Layotte thinks she's all by herself and havin' a cryin' spell. Don't want anyone to know she's feelin' blue."

"But she's got everything!" Eliza pointed out. "Fancy dresses. Pretty face. Best job on the plantation. Wish I could be just like her. What she got to feel sad about?"

"She's a slave," I reminded Eliza. "All slaves got sorrows."

"You got sorrows like Miss Layotte?"

"Sure do."

"What sorrows you got?" Her eyes widened.

"I tell myself most every day what sorrows I got." I sighed. "When I count 'em all up, I heave 'em across the field. Let the crows pick on 'em like old bones. Can't do much about 'em myself."

"What ails you most, Abram?"

"The first one that come to me. My momma dyin' and me never gettin' to meet her. And my daddy runnin' off too."

Eliza sat back on her heels and rocked back and forth.

"I'm luckier than most slaves. Got my

momma and my cousin both . . . but I got sorrows too. I wanna be somebody. Not just do what Master says to do."

My cousin was like a racehorse tied up too long in a barn, stomping its hind legs to get out. Some things are born to run. Not me. I go slow and steady.

It was past dinnertime by then. We both rushed straight back to the trough. We weren't going to get any slice of roast beef or chunk of chocolate cake with butter icing there. I scooped corn mush up with my bare hands and poked Eliza in the ribs to do the same. She turned her nose up at it. She needed this too, I told her. Besides, I didn't want anyone thinking Eliza was getting fed elsewhere. We all had to be the same in the slave quarters or there'd be trouble.

I'd seen the sidelong looks already. New slaves bought at auction stared at Eliza. They drove here in wagons off the beaten road that ran past the cotton fields on Turner's plantation. Sometimes they traveled all the way from South Carolina. But mostly they were sent from nearby towns to be sold at the auction block a few miles away. Such folks wondered. We had all shades of color in the quarters: ink black of the old ones, baked brown of some, honey yellow of others, and then Eliza's pale skin, with blue eyes no slave had. We all knew the way it was here on this plantation. Maybe some never seen it before. I always looked such folks in the eye and planted my feet between them and Eliza like a tree. No one was gonna tell her about her daddy 'cept me.

Granny limped by, squinting at folks eating near the trough. I set a finger on my lips for Eliza to see.

"That you, Abram?" she asked one field worker.

"No, m'am. It's Henry."

Granny stumbled away. She was losing her eyesight along with everything else. Most days, she said clouds covered everything. All she saw was shadows. Her eyes shone bright in her bony face though. She was busy searching for the devil, afraid she'd bump into him.

I had to slip away from her. Just this once.

I shushed Eliza as we backed away from the trough. It was Saturday night, and somewhere folks were meeting, and somewhere they were dancing too. But I had a place to run to now. Drumbeats pounded from across the quarters. Maybe tonight, the men would let me bang their drums again. Maybe tonight, I'd sound just like them.

Chapter 9

Dodo, Dodo Petit

A few months later was the fourth and last hoeing. The first bolls poked their heads up, looking to be picked. When I trudged home from the fields one July day, Eliza was waiting for me.

"They promised me!" she called out to me. "Something special for me today!"

My cousin jumped to her feet. Green onions tumbled out of her apron. On the ground, young 'uns braided garlic into bunches for drying. My cousin's long legs darted off across the yard like sunbeams you couldn't catch. Minutes afterward, we stood in the backyard, our hearts drumming fast. Master's girls were waiting.

Eliza stepped straight up to them with a big grin. She flipped an acorn into the air, caught it, then kneeled to the ground. She flashed that nut from hand to hand quick as mosquito wings. Master's girls could hardly keep their eyes on it whizzing by.

"Guess which hand got it," Eliza demanded.

"Right hand!" Miss Abigail announced.

"Left hand!" snapped Miss Emma.

"Just one guess!" I stepped up.

Miss Abigail looked at me like I was a fly she was gonna swat.

"Right one!" She decided for herself and Miss Emma too.

Just the way Eliza held her head high let me know the answer. She opened her right hand. Empty. Then slowly she turned her left hand over. The acorn was squeezed inside.

"My turn!" cried Miss Emma. "I'm going to watch it close."

I shook my head. Both those girls were studying Eliza like she'd captured a treasure in her hands. All over the yard lay their toys: soft white dolls in dresses, a tea party set, and jump ropes. But they were dying to win at a game we all played in the quarters with sticks and seeds we found on the ground. Eliza was right. Those girls were not happy with anything they had.

I stood with my hat in my hands while they played. Only once did they guess right.

Soon as they won, the game was over.

"Bring me my doll!" Miss Abigail ordered Eliza. My cousin ran for it in a breath. But each time she brought Miss Abigail something, that Master's girl wanted something else.

"Come here, girl!" she bossed Eliza.

My blood was boiling. I hadn't brought Eliza for this. Her next words cut my breath off.

"Know what I always wanted to ask you . . ." sneered Miss Abigail. "Where did you get those blue eyes? No slave's got such eyes."

Eliza jerked like someone slapped her. She stepped back some from Miss Abigail.

"And why aren't you black like Abram," that white girl hissed, "if you're cousins?"

Miss Emma gasped. She looked over her shoulder toward the big house. She reminded me of her momma, Master's wife, her face always hidden by a parasol, her voice honey sweet. Such folks got no say. But Miss Abigail's sharp nose pointed straight toward Eliza like a finger. She reminded me of a hissing goose. I stepped up. So did Miss Layotte, right beside me. I was about ready to yank my cousin away when I heard Miss Layotte say, "Girls, it's about time for your tea party. Gettin' dark, and if you still want to eat some sweets, not much time left."

Miss Emma grabbed Eliza's hand and skipped over to the table where molasses cookies lay beside a pitcher of fresh milk. Her older sister followed them and sat down. Soon the girls were busy at their tea party. I noticed behind Miss Abigail's back how Miss Emma slipped a cookie into Eliza's pocket. No one saw but me.

Words were busting out of me. I could barely keep my mouth shut.

"Miss Abigail is the boss same as the Master," warned Miss Layotte at my side. "He listens to all she says."

The nanny was studying me close, her eyes full on me, not snapping anymore, but glowing warm.

"Look how she's teasin' the girl!" I exploded. "Be glad if she cries. Make her think about things I don't want her to think about."

"Eliza's smart. Near nine. She's gonna figure things out."

"I know I can be a bossy old rooster about Eliza," I confessed as we sat down together.

"Did you learn that from your momma?" The nanny leaned closer to me.

"My momma never had the chance to teach me anything." I swallowed hard. "She died birthin' me. If it weren't for Granny, I wouldn't be here."

"That mumbly, grumbly, old woman?" mocked Miss Layotte. "How did she ever help you?"

"Granny held me screamin' and scrawny in her arms and told Master she needed a boy to help her."

"You're not scrawny, Abram." She smiled at me. "You got big muscles."

Something flashed over me, starting with my face, then across my cheeks until it burned my ears. I kept my eyes to the ground while Miss Layotte went on.

"Sometimes I see you at the far end of the orchard. Eliza ridin' your shoulders and you runnin' so whisper fast, just like a bird. Not even breathin' hard although you're talkin' the whole way."

Neither of us knew where to look then. Suddenly my hands seemed too big. I stuffed 'em into my pockets, but they didn't fit inside.

Miss Layotte's long eyelashes touched her cheek.

"I remember my momma. She was a Creole nanny for a French family. Had a singin' voice like honey. Trained me to be a nanny like her. Just when she trained me good, I was sold to the Turners."

She began to hum a tune, looking up to the sky. "She used to sing to put me to sleep."

> Do-do, do-do pe-tit.
> Do-do pe-tit a moin.
> Sleep, sleep lit-tle one.
> Sleep my lit-tle one.

"I'll never see her again." The nanny sighed. "I got nothin' to hold on to any-more."

I was thinking, at least she got the chance to hear her momma sing. But I didn't tell her that.

"Folks all around here if we want 'em," I told her instead. "I got Eliza to mind. My aunt and Granny watch over me."

"I never seen your aunt. She must be most busy. But I seen your granny. Fussin' and frettin'. Scowlin' all the time."

"How do you know what she does?"

"Oh, I seen her come for the milk each morning early. She looks like an old dried-up apple on a stick."

I had to laugh.

"Know what she says about you?" I teased. "Says you sing devil songs 'cause you're Creole."

"Granny's from old times. All filled up

with the devil and darkness. Afraid to let the sun in. You ever heard her laugh?"

"Naw. She don't laugh. Ever."

Just then, a horse neighed nearby. I jumped quick behind the oak tree. Eliza was busy grooming Miss Abigail, winding stray pieces of her blond hair back into ringlets.

"Looks like my two girls have their own lady in waitin'!" Master's voice boomed across the yard. "Miss Layotte tells me how nice you play, girl. Come along every night. It's alright with me."

"Papa," begged Miss Emma, "can Eliza come live with us?"

Master roared like a lion and slapped his hands on his legs.

"You got your nanny and six maids a-waitin' on you, and now you want this girl too?"

"She does all we say, Papa," the oldest sister reported.

"That's what slaves are good for, Abigail. You just play with her every night, and then we'll see about bringin' her up to our house. Maybe when you have children, she could be their nanny."

Those girls screamed and rushed around their daddy like dandelion seeds blowing in the wind.

"Miss Layotte," announced the Master,

"you've been trainin' this here girl right nice."

His horse trotted off. I leaned against the tree, cussing Master under my breath. All he saw in Eliza was work.

"We got something special for you like we promised!" called Miss Abigail's voice.

I peeked around the tree. A dress was laid out, a golden linen dress with long sleeves, frills at the wrist to keep hands from freckling, and a stand-up collar. Eliza's face was all lit up.

"My momma said to give it to you." Miss Abigail handed my cousin the dress. "We've outgrown it."

From across the yard, I saw Miss Layotte frown. Something she once said thundered loud in my mind. "You take something from the white miss, and you'll be beholdin' to her. That Miss Abigail wants everybody to bow down to her. Got no heart in her body at all. Just be a boss."

Eliza held up the dress like a question for me to answer.

"Go ahead, Eliza," I muttered.

Eliza twirled like a spinning top with that dress hugged close to her chest. Miss Abigail pulled her sister toward the big house. It was long past dusk. Miss Emma squeezed Eliza's hand before she left. When we were alone, Miss Layotte offered me some chocolate cake. I wouldn't touch it. My belly had churned around until it was sour. But Eliza gulped down a fat slice in no time.

"Stop worryin' about your cousin," Miss Layotte scolded me. "I'm trainin' her to be a nanny just like my momma taught me. Someday she'll be free of work in the quarters."

That brightened me up a bit. Working at the big house as a nanny. Eliza was born to it. Even Master had said it.

Chapter 10

Sometimes I'm Up, Sometimes I'm Down

I was changing most every day. At fifteen, I was so tall, only a few men in the quarters were taller and then by only a thumb's length. Hair sprouted up in places it'd never been before. I was still skinny, but around my bone was twisted muscle now, like strong rope. My arms didn't get tired in the fields anymore, but my thoughts circled round and round Miss Layotte like a honeybee. Each week, I wondered if I should go to the dance.

I wished I could ask Granny about Miss Layotte. Granny had been looking at me sidelong, but she held her tongue each night when I ran off to the big house. She never asked me where I was going.

"Granny," I sweettalked her one night after dinner, "let me help you clean up."

I scrubbed the trough clean while Granny poured water into it.

"You know that nanny can sing?" I baited Granny.

"What she sing?" she demanded.

"Singin' about havin' nothin' just like us."

"Devil's song!" hissed Granny. "She's workin' some spell on you. She got mixed-up blood in her."

"You mean like Eliza?" I shot back at her.

Granny scowled. "Got French blood, white blood, and slave blood, all boilin' up inside her. Those Creoles touched by the devil."

"You don't even know her!" I burst out. "She's been feedin' Eliza most every night from Master's table. Trainin' her to be a nanny too. Master approves."

Granny had heard enough. She gathered up her gingham skirts and hobbled across the yard with her cane, stirring up squawking chickens underfoot every which way.

I heard her cussing as she went, "They all no good up at that big house!"

I ran to the breeding cabin next, where Aunt Charity was sweeping dirt out the door. I didn't hear her singing about grace or glory anymore. She was mostly quiet nowadays. She forgot to tie her hair up in rags at night. It hung down loose in her face.

"Is Granny always right?" I skidded to a stop in front of her.

Aunt Charity's broom froze in midair. She set it down and laughed, her big shoulders shaking. She hadn't smiled in a long while.

"Granny believes what she believes. She sees some things different than we do. Doesn't mean she's right. Just means it's the way she thinks."

"She's not right about Miss Layotte, then?"

I felt heat burning my cheek and probably turning me red as an autumn leaf.

"You mean tellin' you to stay away from her?" She stared at me.

I nodded.

"Granny was born on this plantation. Never liked strangers. Watched a heap of slaves come and go. Folks got to prove to her they are hardworkin' like her."

"She doesn't give Miss Layotte a chance."

"Don't give anybody a chance. Too busy givin' orders."

I stuffed my hands so deep in my pockets, my pants almost slid off my hips. I was busy worrying about the dance and whether to go or not. My aunt stepped up close to me. I felt her fingers smooth down the curls that grew wild as weeds on my head.

"She's a kind nanny from what I see.

Good to my Eliza. Sweet to you too. Don't worry what Granny says."

"It's alright, then, my visiting her?"

"I'm pleased you got a friend, Abram."

"But should I go to the dance?" I blurted out.

"All the young folks run to the dance come Saturday night. Nothin' special for you to go. Got music there gonna make you smile and forget all about yourself."

I felt something leap inside me. Nothing could stop me from going to the dance that night. But I had to step across the quarters first to wash at the stream and change clothes in the cabin. I bumped into Granny again.

Granny was bent down on her knees in the dirt by the trough. She couldn't get up if no one was around to help her, but she prayed that way all the same. She rocked back and forth with her eyes closed. Her voice came deep from her belly in low bass notes.

Down on me. Down on me.
Looks like ev-er-y bo-dy in the
whole world's down on me.
Some-times I'm up. Some-times I'm down.
Some-times I'm al-most on the ground.

I remembered how Eliza was so surprised

I had troubles, and now I felt the same, listening to Granny.

Hea-ven's so high.
I am so low.
Don't know if I'll e-ver get to hea-ven or no!

"You ailin', Granny?"

She opened her eyes, and for the first time, she looked peaceful, not scowling mad.

"Just tellin' my troubles to God. Makes me forget 'em."

"What do you do when the troubles come?"

"Busy myself with babies and cookin' and bossin' and soon enough I'm tearin' up all over the place. Forget all my sorrows."

"You sad about being a slave?" I asked.

"Been a slave all my eighty-two years. Born into it." Granny shook her head. "All I know is work. Ain't no way out of it now."

I reached out my hands when she stirred and let her lean on me to stand. A million lines crumpled her face. I set her cane in her left hand and watched as she wobbled off.

"Comin' to the end of my time, Abram," she called back. "Be most happy when I go."

I'd been with Granny every day of my fifteen years. I mostly forgave the way she was. If Granny wouldn't like Miss Layotte, I had to let it be. But I felt sorry for her believing there was no way out.

Chapter 11

Reelin' and A-rockin'

I begged Eliza a hundred times to smooth those curls of mine 'til all the knots came free. I slipped into a clean shirt. I had pressed it between layers of burlap the night before and slept on top of it. I didn't bother with shoes. They never fit me anyhow. Before Eliza could ask me when I was coming home, I flew out the door.

The workers said the meeting place was down in the bottoms somewhere. Here and there in the damp earth of the swamp pressed footprints of bare feet traveling north. I followed them. No stars shone. I was so lit up inside, I didn't need much light anyway.

I must have glowed like a firefly flitting by.

I knew when I came to it. Such a racket shook out of the bush, I thought the trees would keel over. Willows bent to the ground, listening. I peeped through the clearing. It was just a shed for pigs that nobody used anymore, half falling down and leaning to the ground. Music shouted out of it so loud, seemed it would knock the rest of that shed down.

A coffee-skinned man met me at the door.

"Where you from, son?"

"Turner's."

A long row of boys leaned against the wall like a line of skinny scarecrows, and I leaned with them. Our hands were sunk into our pockets, and our eyes stared straight ahead. I recognized some of 'em, but most were strangers from plantations on the other side of the field somewhere.

At the other end were the musicians, shaking dry gourd rattles, tapping bones on a tin pot, and yanking strings stretched over a log of hollow wood. There was booming from the drummers, clanging, and slamming their palms flat on drums: finger drums, long log drums. *Rat-a-tat-tat!* Those drummers carried the beat so loud, you just had to listen. It shot up through your legs straight into your belly. To all that singing and stringing, folks were dancing or standing, moving in time with it.

I had to tap my feet or they'd start jumping by themselves.

Wake up Jo-nah, you are the man!
Reel-in' and a-rock-in' on the ship so tong!

The song carried me like Ben's voice carried us all in the fields, pushing us through
heat-heavy afternoons, so we didn't feel the
pain anymore but only the music going
down deep, deep, deeper.

Let's search this ship from bot-tom to top!
Found bro-ther Jo-nah ly-in' fast a-sleep.
Reel-in' and a-rock-in' on the ship so long!

"Slaves all in the belly of the whale," said
the coffee-skinned man beside me when
the music stopped. "But didn't Jonah get
free?"

I remembered learning about this man
Jonah from Granny. How he was swallowed
by the whale and lay in his belly for a long
while, near dead, but waiting to get free.

"Do any of us get out?" The words leaped
out of me.

"Sure do." He nodded. "Some run so fast,
the hounds can't catch 'em. Call 'em runaways."

Runaways! That's what my daddy had

done. He ran off where nobody could find him, not even me.

"Where do they go?" I yanked his sleeve hard.

"Maybe they made it to Canada. Maybe not." He sighed. "At least they ran free. Got to be brave."

Nobody told me my daddy was brave. Runaway was all I heard about him. Seemed like a bad name. I thought he just ran off and left us. I didn't know he was looking for something. Freedom.

"But there's another way to get out." The man smiled.

My eyes fixed on him, studying his secrets.

"Folks up and down this country plottin' to free slaves." He leaned close to my ear. "It happens here and there."

"How?"

"Some man bought up a slave at the auction last month and set him free."

I must of stood there with my mouth hanging open like a barn door. Just then, the music started up again. We both turned to look.

Folks stepped to the middle of the dirt floor, kicking their shoes off as they went. All the girls wore dresses. I don't know where they got them from. I supposed they were bits and pieces of blankets sewn together. They tied red ribbons in their hair too. Men wore clean shirts. Women set their hands on their hips as their skirts swirled. Men just grinned and twirled them around.

Bare feet slapped against the hard dirt ground. Hands clapped to the beat.

Wake up Jo-nah, you are the man!
Reel-in' and a-rock-in' on the ship so long!

And there in the middle of the floor danced Miss Layotte without a partner. She didn't wear starched clothes. She wore a red gingham dress that just brushed her thighs like she'd outgrown it. How it swirled and jumped with her! For the first time, I saw her hair loose, honey brown curls trickling down her neck. She had her hands on her hips and whizzed in circles. The coffee-skinned man walked over and placed a full glass of water on top her head. Folks backed off the dance floor to make room for a contest.

"She's gonna set the flo!" someone shouted. "Dance the song through without spillin' any water or tumblin' the glass."

Miss Layotte's body swayed from side to side like she had no backbone at all. Her legs

114

jumped high. The arch of her foot lifted nimble as a snake. Such slender legs she had. Around and around in circles she whirled. Her neck veins popped and pulsed. She was covered with sweat and wouldn't look at anyone, just kept dancing is all. When the music ended, the coffee-skinned man lifted the glass of water off her head and held it high. Full of water it was. Not one drop had spilled.

The crowd cheered and clapped. Miss Layotte bowed low. When she stood up, she looked straight at me, shining like the sun, chest heaving, she was so breathless. Such a smile I never saw before, dazzling bright. Then she took a step toward me.

I hung my head down and stepped back some. I didn't know what such a pretty girl wanted from a boy like me. Before I could stop myself, I slipped out the back door and ran back across the bottoms. Midnight dew lay heavy on the bushes. The perfume of jasmine flowers spun so sweet on the air, but it just ached inside me.

Chapter 12

No More Rain
Fall to Wet 'Em

Spring mornings in those fields, all we heard was cries from the oak tree, babies wailing after their mommas. I bit my lip, then tried singing to block out their screams. Workers hit hoes hard to the dirt, metal ringing in our ears. But soon all of us were listening to it again. Seven babies were nursing. The only time it was quiet was noon when the women nursed 'em till they dozed off. By afternoon, when the sun warmed 'em and flies buzzed in their faces, those babies woke with an awful fretting.

Who'd let a baby cry like that? You've got to pick 'em up and rock 'em. That's what we did in the quarters. But we couldn't go to 'em. Not me, once a breeding-cabin boy, and not their daddies, working beside me, busting to go. Not even their own mommas, who stood stiff as if they'd been kicked, could go.

"That's my Sally Ann," a woman sighed. "She's got a pricklin' heat rash."

Or, "Don't cry Moses. Please, baby!"

They'd whisper it low 'cause the overseer would swing on by with his whip if he heard. But those babies couldn't hear anyone a half mile across the field. Overseer had carved out the middle of a rotten log like a long cradle and set them inside. They couldn't crawl anywhere if they wanted to. Their mommas set 'em inside come dawn and ran back to 'em at noon.

Came a thunder and lightning one day like the end of the world. A spring storm rode in like a surprise. It grabbed us so quick, we didn't know it was coming. One minute, a cloud sailed from the north, and by the next breath, it was on top our heads, purple mad. Thunder growled and lightning lit the field so, it near blinded us. Raindrops stabbed our skin like a thousand knives. We couldn't even see where we were at. Couldn't run for cover either. We hid our faces under our arms. Quick as it began, it stopped.

One mother bolted across the field though it wasn't allowed. The others ran after her to the oak tree. Hoes flew in the air behind them. There came a screaming that curdled my blood. It sounded like a pack of wild animals let loose. We all stopped picking to look up. Mothers lifted their limp babies to the sky and shook them hard.

Overseer rode over to them and cursed, "What's this fussin' about?"

"They all dead!" they wailed. "Drowned in their cradle!"

That cradle had filled with rainwater so fast, those babies were covered with water from head to toe. By the time the mothers arrived, they were floating facedown, dead. All seven of 'em.

I lowered my head and scraped the endless weeds, hoping everyone would fall in line. I heard the mumbling behind me and praying under our breath for those babies' souls. Some had been baptized in the mileback stream. Some had not. Overseer tore up the field with his whip, ordering the women to carry their dead babies back to the quarters and bury 'em.

"Shove 'em all in the same hole and get back to work!"

When Master drove by later, his face looked just like storm clouds, dark and ready to burst. There were no tears in his eyes like there were in ours. He dragged that cradle away with a rope tied to the back of

118

his horse, stirring up mud as he rode off. He cussed all the way back across the field.

Late that night, when the big house was dark, we all met at the back of the quarters, field workers, breeders, and house slaves too. Miss Layotte stepped forward and handed seven black satin ribbons to the mothers one by one. She left me a woolen blanket for Granny too.

Folks gathered in a circle around a wide hole dug that morning, Some men held pine torches high. I didn't want to, but I had to look down. Inside, seven babies were laid side by side, wrapped in white muslin, heads touching. Their eyes shut tight like they were asleep.

Beside me, Granny just shook her head and stood silent. My aunt held back one of the mothers from dropping down into the pit. All I could do was squeeze Eliza's hand tight in mine.

One of the fathers walked past us and leaned over the grave. His skin was so black it shone under the torchlight. He laid a bow with seven arrows across the babies' chests and left a tiny wooden canoe with seven paddles too.

"To protect you on your journey home," he spoke to them. "To slay any enemies on your way across the waters."

"You'll be back where you belong," said his wife. "In Africa, where we were free."

One by one, the mothers tucked a sack of cornmeal beside each baby for the journey. Around me, folks called out their good-byes as they threw a handful of dirt over the babies.

"Speed your way," said one.

"Be safe," wished another.

As I threw my handful of dirt, I closed my eyes. I pictured the babies in their canoe, backs to us, heads looking toward Africa.

"Go home now," I whispered.

Drumbeats tapped, soft and low like heartbeats. Ben started humming. I knew the tune, a mourning song. I'd heard it sung at funerals before.

When old folks died, mostly you were glad for them. Sometimes we danced at their leave-taking. They had a better place to go. But the singing was bitter that night and broken by weeping. I could not open my mouth to join in.

No more rain fall to wet you.
No more sun shine to burn you.
No more part-ing in the king-dom.
Ev-e-ry day shall be Sun-day.

The slaves hummed that song all night

long, their heads down, arms wrapped around the children they had left. By midnight, it was the only sound I heard in my head.

No more rain fall to wet you.
No more sun shine to burn you.

At last, the tiny grave was covered. We all trudged home to our cabins. "Gone to God." Granny's words did not help us. Eliza sat up for the longest time in a dark corner of the cabin. She would not eat one bite of dinner. I wrapped my arms around my cousin and rocked her. There was nothing to say and nowhere to look except up to the night sky. We kept waiting for the stars to come out, but they never did.

The next morning, my aunt had to tug me out of bed. In the field, no one sang any work songs. No one shouted greetings across the rows. There was silence except for the far-off calls of toddlers. The mothers turned their heads and frowned each time they screamed. They hoed without looking, slicing cotton plants down to the ground.

"Hush now!" one mother called out to them. "Wait till noon. We'll come by same as always."

Then I felt a stirring in the field like birds flapping their wings and lifting off. A rustle came from a row farther off across the field than I could see.

Words were whispered into the air, and they sent a shiver right through me:

"Boss am comin'! Boss am comin'!"

From mouth to mouth, it rolled down the rows like a drumbeat.

"Boss am comin'! Boss am comin'!"

Those who began the chant were quiet and staring at their hoes when Master appeared. He hardly ever rode down the rows. But he was not alone. Eliza trailed behind his horse, a water bucket in each hand, pockets bulging with cornpones. She stumbled as she walked, spilling drops from each pail.

"Careful, girl."

Master turned to look behind him. He noticed me staring.

"You, boy, get over here and help this child out."

I ran over, fingers trembling, and lifted the buckets from my cousin's hands.

"I can't spare any breeding women to care for the children in these fields," Master's voice boomed. "You're gonna feed the children at noon from now on."

"Yes, sir!" Eliza immediately shot back at him.

"Gonna bring the breeder's children out here too. You gonna remember to run for 'em in the rain and feed 'em come noon?"

"Yes, sir!"

"Guard those babies close. Come at noon. Stay with 'em all afternoon." He looked down from his horse. "You better live up to all Miss Layotte says about you."

"I will, sir!"

Around us, workers hacked weeds double fast until the Master rode off and disappeared in the sun-bright field. Then they set their hoes down and stared at us. From far off, the conker shell blew five times. All the workers hurried over to us.

"Our young 'uns will be safe now." One mother smiled.

We squatted out of the wind to nibble on cornpones and swallow dips from the drinking bucket. Eliza leaned close to me.

"You just wait," she promised. "Those babies gonna grow up strong and listen good. I'll train 'em just right."

"Granny sure will be pleased," I told her.

"She's been a fine granny to us," sighed my cousin. "Taught you and me most everything."

Eliza was right. She wouldn't be here minding babies if not for Granny's training. My cousin was just nine years old and already taking charge. Granny could rest easy.

Soon newborns were wiggling on and off Eliza's lap, too many of 'em to even count. Fists yanked her braids. Fingers poked into her mouth. They clung to her like she was their momma. Each week it seemed another one was born in the breeding cabins. More got to stay with us now instead of getting sold away. Master needed to make up for the seven he lost.

"They all the time hungry." Eliza shook her head one noon. "Cry even in their sleep. Got no daddy to love 'em, and their momma's all the time busy."

Eliza patted their backs some, and they got still, sat on their bottoms, and looked up at her with wide eyes.

"How do you know to quiet 'em down so?" I wondered.

"Why, Abram," Eliza fixed one saucy blue eye on me, "I fuss with 'em like you fussed with me. Don't you remember?"

"I had just one baby," I laughed, "not a heap like you got."

But we didn't sit too long 'cause the over-seer passed by to make sure we weeded the rows. I whispered to Eliza before filing back to the field with the others, "Round up the young 'uns to rest under the bushes. They'll sleep sound with that warm milk in their bellies."

Eliza gathered all the children crawling here and there in those fields of cotton. The sun was so bright, you couldn't even see. Everything was glaring white. It was hard to keep track of those young 'uns. Eliza scooped them into her arms just like I used to scoop her up. She rocked the babies back and forth, back and forth. If I stood real quiet in that shimmering, hot field, I heard her voice, light and cool, telling stories to set them to sleep, singing lullabies I once sung to her. Soon all those babies were yawning.

Who all the time a-hid-in'
in the cot-ton and the corn?
Mam-my's lit-tle ba-by,
Mammy's lit-tle ba-by.
Who all the time a-blow-in'
old Mas-ter's din-ner horn?
Mam-my's lit-tle ba-by,
Mammy's lit-tle ba-by.

My fingers whirred in and out of the bushes quick as hummingbird wings, as I listened to her.

Then a stillness came, a noontime stillness. All of 'em were asleep, Eliza too.

Chapter 13

How Long Before the Sun Goes Down?

Summer evenings, we'd pick 'til last light, but the young 'uns headed back to the quarters with Eliza come three blows of the conker shell. They all ate dinner squirming around the trough. Eliza tore a storm across that field, spreading a trail of dust behind her. The oldest children chased after her, carrying the few babies she couldn't. She had places to go. She'd run to Granny and set a cool cloth on her head, then check to see what her momma needed done. She jumped around the quarters like a leapfrog. She'd be in such a hurry to get to the big house.

Just before she ran off one night, she looked at me and said, "You figure on going to the dance come Saturday?"

The dance was all I thought about lately. "I'm thinkin' on it."

"You never did say how you liked it."

"Sure was lively." I had to grin. "Best part was the drums. You don't have a choice but to sing and dance when you hear 'em."

"You saw Miss Layotte there?"

"She was settin' the flo'. Best dancer there."

"But you didn't dance with her!" She set her hands on her hips.

"Why . . . how do you know?"

"She told me, just as she was headin' for you, you slipped out the door."

I picked double time, my fingers hopping fast as fleas in and out of the bushes.

"Miss Layotte's gonna ask me when I come by later if you plan on going," Eliza demanded. "What should I tell her?"

My heart drummed in my chest to remember Miss Layotte. I'd seen a slave girl stuff wild rose petals into her bosom one Saturday night and wondered if that's what the nanny did too.

"Tell her I'm thinkin' on it, girl!"

My cousin flopped her arms down to her sides and took off, running so fast she stirred the crows up. Crows sailed above her head across the field, squawking loud and bold.

Caw! Caw! Caw!

She skipped lively to the beat of the

crowsong, her head waving from side to side, as if she were going somewhere besides the flat mile back to the quarters.

The next day, Eliza wore the linen dress Miss Abigail gave her. My aunt helped her dress, then set a floppy straw hat on her head, and tucked my cousin's wavy black hair underneath.

I kept my lips shut tight when Eliza showed up that afternoon. But that evening, I walked straight to the breeding cabins. My aunt was brewing bitter herbs in a big pot.

"What are you dressin' Eliza like that for?" I demanded.

"What do you mean, boy?" my aunt shot back at me.

Her face was pinched tight as a thunderbolt ready to explode.

"That's a Sunday dress." I stamped my foot down.

Men went to the field barechested, barefooted, with a wide hat. Women wore loose sacks to catch a breeze and calico head scarves.

"You dressin' her like a white girl!" I shouted.

"Look at that pale skin of hers," she pleaded. "Not dark like ours. She's gonna fry out there if I don't cover her up. Not enough shade for miles around."

Aunt Charity came over to me then and set her hands on my shoulders. Instead of the storm I was expecting, tears shone like raindrops in her eyes.

"Let her be, Abram." She sighed. "She's gonna have a hard life ahead. We got to make it easy for her, long as we can."

I clamped my mouth shut. Aunt Charity was right. She took everything easy and slow. Not like me. I was always too serious.

It's just that I saw things most folks don't. Sometimes I'd look up to see a carriage drive by slow on the beaten road. White folks shaded their brows for a closer look at the half-white girl in a fancy dress. Slaves were supposed to be all bent over, bony and ugly, working cotton under the blasted sun. But Eliza'd be tiptoeing in her bare feet, swinging toddlers high in the air and catching them up in her arms.

Sometimes, in the evenings, she danced while the men drummed in the quarters. I wondered where she'd learned that fancy stepping, but I never asked. For, once I set my hands on those log drums, I never thought about much.

It was hard keeping up with my cousin in those days. She was always up before me, tickling me awake with her fingertips buzzing across my face like a thousand flies and rushing me out the door. Though it was still dark, Eliza beamed bright as noonday sun. When she showed up at feeding time, she looked across the cotton fields and admired 'em. She didn't see the backs bent to the sun, half of us broken down.

"It's endless!" she gasped. "Rows long and straight. All that brown dotted with white. Must reach to the next county."

I stared down the rows, thinking how I didn't see the beauty anymore.

"The world's so big out here! No end to it," she exclaimed. "In the quarters, no room for anybody."

It was different for me. Out in the fields, I felt just like the cotton. Trapped in a cage. Summer nights, I couldn't go home until the moon climbed high in the sky. We picked under its light until Ben headed us home. All afternoon I heard my partner wail.

How long be-fore the sun goes down?
I wish I had a-died when I was young.
I ne-ver would a-had this race to run
be-fore the sun goes down.

But we still had the night to pick after that. When we walked back at last, I felt like I was falling asleep on my feet. Slaves stumbled past, too tired to wave good night. Aunt Charity was already asleep, and Granny was snoring. Only Eliza would be awake, propped up on her elbows, waiting on me.

Those moments between dark and falling asleep were all the time I had to keep track of my cousin. We had some time together at noon, but I mostly drifted off in the heat. Sometimes I'd call to her across the field while I picked, but that overseer had ears like a wild animal stalking prey. I swore he heard my thoughts whisper in my head.

Night is the time for talking anyway. Day is done. The day stretched behind us like a long road we didn't have to walk anymore. It was just the two of us then, sitting up, backs pressed against the cabin wall, watching the moon light up our window.

"Miss Layotte's been askin' for you," she blurted out right off. "I tell her you're chained to the fields and can't come see her."

I thought back to the dance and how, if I'd been brave like my daddy, I would have stepped right up to Miss Layotte and danced with her.

"You love runnin' up to the big house, don't you girl?"

Eliza's forehead was wrinkled. I knew that

look. Her momma wore it all the time now.

"Miss Layotte's always kind to me. Teachin' me how to take care of Master's girls. Whisperin' in my ear what to do. But . . ."

"What do you talk to Miss Emma about?"

"We got plenty to say." A smile flashed over her face. "She asks if I can tell what the weather's supposed to be. Hangs on all I say."

"And Miss Abigail?"

Eliza took a breathlong pause and frowned most hard.

"Just listen to her is all. Miss Layotte says I got to watch my words. But Miss Abigail all the time teases me cause I got blue eyes."

"Don't pay her any mind."

"Abram," her lips trembled, "nobody, even my momma, ever did tell me about . . . my daddy."

I was almost dead asleep on the floor, but that woke me.

"I asked Granny who my daddy is. She told me how she named you Abram from the Bible. Means 'father of us all.' Said my having you was enough. But do you know who my daddy is?"

I knew it was gonna come one day. It was like being trapped on a dead-end road.

"All my life I wondered who my daddy was too," I confessed.

132

"But you know he was a slave from this plantation," she spoke up. "He must of loved your momma before he ran away."

"I never met him. I don't know where he's at."

"I don't know nothin' about my daddy! All I know is I was born with blue eyes and light brown skin." She stared at me. "You gonna tell me the reason why?"

"We got all shades of color livin' in the quarters," I told her. "Black. Coffee. Tan. No tellin' what color we are born with."

Eliza grabbed both my hands and pulled me up from the floor.

"Tell me the truth!"

"It's . . . Master Turner!"

I spit the name into the air like a curse. My stomach knotted up to think of that man. My cousin wrapped her arms around her chest and rocked back and forth in a tight ball.

"Your momma had no choice, girl!" I insisted.

"He's not my daddy! Don't even look at me. Cussin' all the time at my momma." Her mouth shut in one tight line.

We sat without saying a word for a long time. It was so quiet, I could hear a ball of sweat roll down my neck.

Next thing I knew, she was leaning against

me, tears storming out of her. I rocked her back and forth like a baby, 'til her eyelids shut and she curled up to sleep. At least, I was the one got the chance to tell her.

I thought how nobody knew much about my daddy. I would never see his face. But if he was willing to run to freedom, he must be a man who believed in things. He wasn't like Master who looked right past us and didn't see us. My daddy must have loved my momma like Eliza said. He would have loved me too if he stayed.

I laid down with my eyes wide open, watching over my cousin. When she was little, she'd sleep on top my chest like a bird in its nest, a burlap sack stretched across us both. I learned not to stir the whole night long so that she could sleep sound.

But now Eliza slept between Aunt Charity and me. We kept her warm from both sides. Both of us were guarding Eliza, holding back the troubles from coming in, as long as we could.

Chapter 14

No Hiding Place

Summer nights last too long for cotton pickers. That's when the overseer drove us to work long past dusk. Past dusk to darkness. Past darkness to midnight. Sometimes, on summer nights, we unloaded our sacks in pitch black. It was hot and still, even on those evenings. The air didn't move all day. Day and night felt just the same. At dinner, we swallowed our cornpone same as we did at lunch, but we didn't get to go home. We headed back to the fields again.

Come late August, that full moon smiled above us like a second sun, lighting up the cotton bright as daylight. I cussed at it as I picked. I never got to the Saturday night dance anymore. I barely made it home by midnight. I couldn't move a muscle, let alone dance.

My fingers snapped up that cotton double speed just to get it over and done with. But there seemed to be no end. I felt as itchy as if a hundred mosquitoes lit on my bare back.

At last, Ben called, "Aah yee hoo!" and my feet ran before I could think. For once, I might make it to the big house with Eliza. I yelled at my partner to unload my sack, and I flew off. One foot was up in the air somewhere, and the other whizzed over the ground. And then it came to me. All this time, I thought it was the food for Eliza I was scrambling for, but my cousin had already up and gone to the big house. That's not what set my heart a-pitter-patter. Miss Layotte was the one I wanted to see.

But it was deep dark, and the yard was empty. No honey sandwich hung in the oak tree. I dragged myself home to the cabin. Eliza sat up alone in the darkness. Aunt Charity and Granny were off at the breeding cabins.

"So many troubles on this plantation." She frowned. "Momma just goes along with 'em and sings hymns."

"We got to have one face to show to Master," I shared my secret. "Another we show to ourselves."

"Everybody does that?"

"All folks do, slaves and masters both. Keeps the peace."

Then she sighed in a dreamy voice, full of sleep. "When I grow up, Miss Layotte says I'll be the nanny to Miss Emma and Miss Abigail's children!"

"You always jumpin' to the next step, Eliza. No stoppin' you. Where you headed next, I wonder?"

I was sure that girl had the sign of luck over her, just like the crows predicted. She wouldn't be a breeder like she feared, and Master didn't push her to pick cotton even in high season when most folks went. Eliza wouldn't like it in the fields anyway. Getting a sack was the beginning and the end. You didn't go any place from there. You just picked your fill until you were too old to move. I'd seen the women who picked cotton all their lives. They were bone-thin like scarecrows. They rose hours before dawn, sleepwalking to the field, and staggered home at dusk to care for their babies.

Eliza had a place to be come day. Nights she ran to the big house without me. But late one moonlit night, when I got home, Eliza was sitting up alone, crying in a dark corner of our cabin.

"We just played tug of war," she confessed. "But I tugged too hard and both girls fell down in the mud. Got their dresses all dirty."

"You just stronger than them 'cause you been a breedin' cabin girl."

"When I helped 'em up, Miss Abigail smacked my face so hard, Miss Emma yelled at her to stop. Her sister told me never to come back again. Said she hated all slaves."

"What did you do?"

"Ran off." She bowed her head. "Miss Emma called and called after me. I could hear her voice all through the orchard."

"Miss Emma wants you back." I nudged her. "She'll beg her daddy to talk to her sister."

"Master don't care. Got a cold heart. Why would he tell Miss Abigail to ask me back?"

I squeezed her hand tight for an answer. She fell asleep curled up tight like Granny.

I didn't tell Eliza how Miss Layotte sneaked into the quarters early that morning and whispered a warning at our window. "Best you keep Eliza away from the big house, Abram!"

"But all Eliza wants is to play with those girls come evenin'."

"Miss Abigail don't want her anymore." She hung her head down.

"What makes that Miss Abigail so mean?"

"Folks whisper how Eliza's the prettiest girl around, but Miss Abigail's plain as a pancake. Fusses to her momma about why some slave's so light skinned. Begs her momma to get rid of Eliza, but her momma just say shush."

Miss Layotte didn't say the rest. But I knew anyway. If Eliza couldn't go to the big house anymore, I couldn't go.

I was gonna have to sneak around. Master had spies everywhere, Granny warned.

"For slaves," Granny said, "there's no hidin' place." I remember her chanting low and deep.

> *I run to the rock*
> *for to hide my face.*
> *The rock cried out,*
> *no hid-ing place!*

Each night, Eliza still ran the extra mile up to the big house and waited behind the oak tree, peeping out every minute. But the yard was empty. The sisters never came by. I begged her to stop running there.

A few days later, Master's family drove past us on the beaten road come noon. From across the field, I felt that white miss stare at us stone-faced. Miss Abigail could have dried up a cotton boll with that look.

Eliza waved, but the sisters never waved back. Eliza stopped still, shading her forehead, and followed them with her eyes a long mile before they disappeared. She hung her head down for days afterwards.

As for me, I couldn't go far. I couldn't do much either. I was chained to that overseer. He pained me. He rode up and down the rows, his hot breath roaring down my back like fire. Stink from his sweat burned into my nose. He was thirsty for blood from a slave's back. He thought with his whip and measured my work to the ounce. If I picked one more sack yesterday, he knew it. If I didn't do the same or better today, that whip flashed out.

I drew my mouth in a straight line and gritted my teeth like Ben taught. That took the first sting away. For the past three years, since I was fifteen, I'd done a man's share. So I had to get used to more pounding on my back.

Twenty-five lashes if you broke a branch.

In the last week of summer, a thunderstorm pelted down on all of us in the field and drenched that cotton through and through. We let go a mighty roar and rushed off the fields, scooping the babies in our arms. It was late on a Saturday.

There was just one place to go.

"C'mon girl. If we're not welcome at the big house anymore," I flew into the cabin, "got a better place to be!"

"Where we goin'?"

I yanked her to her feet.

"Down to the bottoms to dance!" I shouted. "Slip into that golden dress and tie your hair up."

We crept to the bottoms, tiptoeing side by side. Eliza peered through the dark and rain with her face lit up like she was searching for a star dropped down from the sky. We didn't dare breathe or say any more.

Chapter 15

Gonna Shout All Over God's Heaven

I ran across the bottoms, dragging Eliza with me, her breath gasping in my ears. We both felt the ground shake with the boom of drumbeats. Ahead shone a light from one candle. Men stood outside, listening still.

"He's Turner's boy." The coffee-skinned man recognized me. "Seems he brought his sister."

Eliza headed straight to the floor to dance. That shed was jumping. Washboards were strumming. Someone blew on a jug. Bone clappers tapped. And the drummer slapped on a barrel held tight between his knees. It all came together, pounding out the same beat. One man started singing and everybody joined in.

I've got a song. You-ve got a song.

All of God's chil-dren got a song.
When I get to Heav-en,
  gon-na sing a new song.
Gon-na sing all o-ver God's Heav-en!

Workers I had slaved over cotton with ran
to the floor. We had picked side by side for
months, backs bent, whip-burns branding
us, sacks dragging from our shoulders. Not
one word dared we speak. They hardly
looked the same now, jumping and twirling
their girlfriends around. They grinned like
jack-o'-lanterns.

They shouted to the night sky with the
song.

I got shoes! You got shoes!
Gon-na walk all o-ver God's Heav-en!

Shoes flew off folks' feet. The whole shed
seemed to lean one way and then another
way with the beat. The drummer slammed
down hard on his barrel. He closed his eyes
and let that music take him. All around me,
hands clapped to the roll of his drum.
Thump! Thump! Thump! Suddenly the
drummer stood up and pounded the barrel
with the top of his head, his arms swaying
high in the air. *Slam! Slam! Slam! Wham!*
Voices ended in a long hum of breath

stretched out endlessly long.

Gon-na shout all o-ver God's Heav-en-n-n!

I didn't even know it, but I had edged up to that drummer while he was playing. I was so close to him, I breathed in his ear. He reached out and drew me beside him, placing both my hands on the ox hide of his barrel.

"Try it son!" he screamed. "I heard you play in the quarters."

The washboard started up again, squeaking in my ears. Someone blew notes on a jug. *Tap! Tap! Tap!* sounded the bones. And then it was my turn. I slammed my palms flat down. The drummer showed me how to lift my fingers and tap 'em down one after another like running feet and how to slam with the sides of my palms for a slow-me-down. Soon he left me alone. I didn't ask myself what I was doing up there in front of everyone. I didn't pay 'em no mind. Besides, they were busy dancing. So I just drummed.

Behind me, some men were whispering about a Father Johnson up the road a ways. I drummed lighter so I could hear. He was a white man's preacher, but he bought up slaves at auction and set 'em free like the coffee-skinned man once told me. They called him a name: a-bo-li-tionist. A strange name, but the way they said it was like they whispered God's name.

Once I looked up to see Eliza twirling with Miss Layotte, skirts flying in the air, feet sidestepping fancy, and thought the nanny had taught her more than I knew. But mostly I played, listening to drumbeats bang on the air, slamming that hunger clear out of me.

Fire shot through my hands, inside my chest, and up and down my backbone, shooting through me like a lightning bolt.

I kept on.

The musicians slowed down when the coffee-skinned man drew circles on the floor with a charred corncob, and the girls stepped into 'em one by one.

We sped up when he called out, "Cake-walk! Whoever dances longest inside the circle wins a piece of cake. No steppin' on the line!"

I was beating and beating down hard with fingers, palms, and the bones of my hands. I even used my elbows. When I looked up to wipe sweat out of my eyes, I saw just two dancers left, Miss Layotte and a tall girl. The nanny twisted and shimmied inside that circle about the size of a barrel. She kept her feet clean inside it. The tall girl danced a two-step but did no high leaping. She kept her eyes on Miss Layotte and her feet close to the ground. The coffee-skinned man leaned forward, counting out their steps. Miss Layotte jumped high in the air and spun around like a top. I held my breath. She landed back down inside the circle. I thumped my drum. The tall girl leaned back to watch her as she danced. Her heel stepped on the line.

"Out!" shouted the man.

That tall girl frowned and left the floor. All eyes swung back to Miss Layotte. She moved her feet so swift, they were invisible.

"One thousand steps!" the coffee-skinned man yelled out.

Miss Layotte slowed to a chest-heaving stop, breathing from her belly to her throat. She set her hands on her hips and threw her head back. She smiled to the night sky poking in through the rooftop. Afterwards she leaned against the wall to rest. Someone handed her a piece of ginger cake on a plate, stolen from the big house I imagined.

The drummer sat down in my place to play. Couples ran to the dance floor to strut. When I stepped down, my hands vibrated like they were still beating on the drum. Eliza grabbed them hard.

"What are you waitin' for?" she screamed

in my ear. "Go ahead and dance with her!"

I wanted to walk onto the dance floor, but I could not. I dared not even look at Miss Layotte. I was stuck to the ground as if my feet grew roots, the sweat pouring down my back, when I felt Eliza's shove, firm as a horse's hoof against my back. Before I knew it, I was standing in front of the nanny.

"Abram, I never danced like that before!" She touched my arm. "You drummin' up there so wild, my feet couldn't stop."

"But I . . . I didn't know what I was doin'!"

"You're the finest drummer I ever heard. Helped me win the contest."

She split the ginger cake in three and handed one to Eliza, flying by us. The biggest piece she slid into my wide-open mouth. It was spicy sweet. I even licked her fingers some. And then my laughter came shooting out like a spring from deep inside me. Giggles popped out of her throat like high musical notes.

I shuffled backward onto the dance floor and reached out my hands to Miss Layotte. I twirled her around like I'd seen the men do and pulled her close, her head below my chestbone. We spun in circles east and west, whooping and hollering to the music as we danced. Everytime Miss Layotte pressed against me, a cloud of roses drifted up.

Afterward we leaned against the wall together to cool off. I slipped my hand into hers. I was grinning so hard, it hurt my face. For Miss Layotte, the fanciest girl at the dance, leaned on one side of me. And in front of us, my cousin Eliza was swirling, her linen dress flying in a whir of circles.

Heads turned, men and women alike, to look at her.

Since she was born, I thought she was a beauty. Eliza was tall like me, but not skinny, on account of Miss Layotte's handouts. She was round and bright as a harvest moon, with full red lips too. She reminded me of Aunt Charity before her troubles came.

The truth is, she didn't look like any relative of mine. My face kinda hung down long, so I looked sad as a hound dog. I was born into troubles, and they weighed me down. When Eliza danced, she stood straight shouldered, like she was looking her troubles in the eye. Her troubles weren't a part of her, the way they were with me.

I hoped Eliza would never pay any mind to what Granny warned, that her life would be trouble. I wanted her to believe what her momma said, that something good was gonna come out of all her troubles.

Sometime after midnight, we walked

home, my hand tight in Miss Layotte's hand. Eliza rode on top my shoulders, her head plopped against mine, dead asleep. That music seemed to follow us, beating inside our heads, so our feet still skipped in time with it. I tapped on Eliza's flipflopping arms like they were drums and swung Miss Layotte's hand back and forth in mine. We stepped light and free across the bottoms.

Chapter 16

I Done Been Tried

Sometimes we sneaked by the big house on our way home from the field on the longest days of summer and drank from the deep well there. By dusk, we dragged our feet. We couldn't make it to the mile-back stream. Nobody was around to see us anyway.

One evening, Eliza stepped up to the well, her dress soaked with sweat. She tipped her head back and emptied a water bucket over her head. She closed her eyes and let that sweet, cool water swallow her like a pretend bath. At thirteen, Eliza smiled most all the time. For four years, she'd watched over the babies in the field. All the mothers felt at ease. Eliza skipped down the rows come noon, holding her head up high.

She was singing now while she splashed water all over herself.

I done been down and I done been tried.
I been through wat-er and I been bap-tiz-ed!

I was about ready to dip some of that water on myself when I heard the curse.

It come loud and clear, spitting clear.

"What a filthy mess you are, Eliza!"

Miss Abigail stood by the fence, hands on her hips. She didn't come any closer than that. Miss Emma stood in her sister's shadow, head low. My cousin stared down at her old linen dress as if seeing it for the first time, torn and hanging like a rag above her dirty bare feet, then at Miss Abigail's mint-green dress cool as julep.

We hadn't seen much of Master's girls those four years. They were always busy reading and writing. Teachers coming and going. Trips everywhere. Once they disappeared for a month with their momma. They traveled overseas, I heard, and brought home fifty new dresses. Miss Abigail was eighteen now. Her perfume and powder didn't smell sweet like they were supposed to. Stunk worse than sweat.

Miss Abigail leaned over the fence and hissed like a snake, "You'll never wash that color out of your skin no matter how hard you rub. You are dark as this dirt at my boots!"

151

I squeezed Eliza's arm hard as a warning sign to hold her tongue. If a slave talked back to a white person, they were tied to a wall, stretched naked in the hot sun. When their back was burning red, Master said it was ready to be whipped.

"You're a slave!" Miss Abigail spit the words out like a curse. "Sneaking around here like you're the same as us. Sorry we ever played with you. We don't talk to your kind."

She grabbed her sister's arm roughly. Miss Emma turned pale like she was gonna faint. I kept my hands ready to lift her if she fell, but Eliza reached her hand to hold her up first. I couldn't help but see how Miss Emma jumped back like she'd been burned.

"Move on, girl!" Miss Abigail yelled, slapping my cousin's hand away.

Then she marched off, pulling her sister along with her. Eliza stood still as still and stared after them for a long while.

I had known all along about Miss Abigail. All she wanted from my Eliza was for her to be a pet. Better it was over now. I grabbed Eliza's hand and headed towards the cabins. Teardrops spilled down her face, leaving two streaks of dirt.

I brushed my cousin's face dry before going inside. I didn't want her momma to see. Aunt Charity had enough worries. She rushed day and night between the young 'uns breeding and the old ones dying. At least she found a way for Master to keep her. She was in charge of the breeding cabins now that Granny was old and couldn't get out of bed. Granny was curled up on some rags in the corner, her knees tucked into her chest, sleeping most of the day, shivering cold even beneath Miss Layotte's blanket.

But Eliza shoved her face flat against the dirt floor. Like a rain barrel left out too long in the rain, her tears just spilled over.

I whispered to my aunt what had happened. For the first time, I saw the wrinkles lining her face.

"Oh . . . they must know who Eliza's daddy is! They are grown now and figured it out. Those girls ain't gonna stop at nothin' now."

"Eliza knows too."

"Who told her?" she gasped.

"I had to say it. She was waitin' on it."

My aunt glanced down at Eliza crying on the floor. She handed me an empty bucket.

"Fetch me some water from the mile-back stream. I need it for washin' some laundry."

It was near dark, too late for washing clothes. You needed to set them out when the sun was shining. But I grabbed the bucket and left without another word. Outside I tiptoed across the porch and perched beneath a window like a bird. It was full dark. Aunt Charity's voice drifted by, deep and low.

"Lift your head up, girl. You been lookin' at the ground too hard. Won't see nothin' but darkness there. Gotta look up to the sky."

After a long wait, I heard a rustling of skirts as my aunt moved closer to Eliza. She held Eliza in her arms, rocking her back and forth.

"You come into this world with beauty. Take after your aunt, Abram's ma. Thin as a willow reed. Big blue eyes."

I leaned against the cabin wall and thought how my momma and my cousin both were born into troubles.

At last, I heard Eliza sigh.

"Ever since I met Miss Abigail, I just tried to please her."

"No matter if you bent over backward for that girl, it'd never be enough."

"I thought if she liked me enough, I could be somebody."

"You're everything to us, but you'll never be anyone to that girl."

"But why does she pick on me? Is it because I'm Master's daughter?"

Such a silence came. I shivered outside alone on the porch.

"Why did you have his babies?"

I heard a gasp of air, hard and sharp.

"Child, I had no choice."

"Why did you go along?"

"Master said he'd sell me away or whip me, maybe even kill me, if I didn't —"

"Why didn't you ever fight him?"

" 'Cause Master gave me something I wished for — you!"

"Me?"

"He promised I could keep my firstborn. That morning you were born, I laughed and cried for hours, I was so happy. For that one thing he gave me, I obey him."

"Did you never want a real husband to love you or a job up at the big house?"

"I don't wish and hope on things I'll never get," my aunt said.

"Why didn't you ever tell me he was my daddy?"

" 'Cause it's a sorrow. Abram says it's the worst one. I prayed you'd never know."

"I had to know about it. Even if it's a wrong thing he done to you."

"He done it to all of us, child." I heard my aunt crying. "But he hurt you the most."

Chapter 17

Girl in a Guinea Blue Gown

We didn't hang around the back of the big house anymore. But I noticed carryings-on up there one spring a full year later. Master's girls dressed fancy most of the time, wearing velvet skirts with wide circles on the bottom that swayed when they walked. They shaded their soft, white skin beneath parasols and painted something pink on their lips. They were ready for courting, Miss Layotte said.

I sneaked by at full dark and saw it all through the lamplit windows. I came to pick up the parcel Miss Layotte set high in the branches of the oak tree. Sometimes it was still warm. I made sure Eliza ate it before she slept.

One night, something hung dark as a shadow up in the tree. I pulled it down. It was a hollowed out tree stump with a sheep-skin stretched smooth and tight across the top. A drum! I hugged it to my chest like Eliza did the babies. I didn't have to wait for the Saturday night dance to play or beg the men to borrow their drums.

Eliza turned fourteen. Changes come over girls then. She was no longer plump, but stretched out tall, high shouldered, and thin waisted. Busy all the long afternoon with the babies under the oaks. She didn't smile near as much though. She was think-ing deep. That was the only way we were alike, Eliza and me.

Came one Sunday I won't ever forget. That was the only day we could be seen any-where, visiting friends on the next planta-tion or strolling a mile down the beaten road to the church we built of weathered barn wood. That's a day felt like freedom 'cause we could roam off Turner's plantation to see what was down the road. Just before we went to church that morning, we stopped in full daylight by the well, hoping to catch sight of Miss Layotte. Eliza was beside me, gliding like wind. She was that smooth-walking, you didn't even hear her step. She wore a newly spun dress. Midnight blue, Betty called it when she handed it to her. It was a long, guinea blue dress, with indigo and white stripes most slave girls wore. That color lit up Eliza's eyes so that they were bluer than a May sky.

All of us were in a spell looking at Eliza.

"Lookin' good," I joked, and sang a dance tune aloud.

> *I ain't gon-na stay no long-er.*
> *Gon-na pack my bundle and go.*
> *'Cause way o-ver yon-der,*
> * in a guin-ea blue gown,*
> * they got a la-dy I used to know.*

Eliza gave a tiny smile. She looked kind of flushed from September heat. Then we noticed the party of white folks in the backyard, young men mostly, dressed in fine linen suits. It was a courting party, it turned out. They all stopped to stare at us, walking from the well to the road. Not at me. I was twenty, older than them and taller too, but I was invisible. It was my cousin they watched. One blond man stood so close by, Eliza almost brushed him in passing. His mouth fell open watching her, a glass of lemonade held stiffly in his hand.

"Who is that pretty girl?" he gasped.

We heard Miss Abigail snap back, her words cold and hard as snake bites, "That's a slave girl! She's always pretending to be white."

"But she's near enough the same color as me!" the blond man protested. "Beautiful blue eyes too. Where did she get them?"

There was a pause. The men in the courting party stared back and forth from Eliza to Miss Emma.

"Looks almost like a sister of yours," someone joked.

"That's why your daddy is so uncommon rich!" the blond man burst out. "He fathers his own slaves! Ought to be a law against it."

I was close enough to see Miss Abigail whirl on her heels and head straight for the house, stirring up big storm clouds of dust. She squeezed Miss Emma's arm and dragged her behind. Eliza turned away, her back straight and her eyes on the road. She didn't look back this time at the white girls or at Miss Layotte running after them. I was the only one to notice how her shoulders trembled in front of me at church. But she never said anything about what happened.

Something felt different in the quarters that evening. Usually, Sunday nights, we strolled from cabin to cabin visiting 'cause we weren't working the fields. But that night, there was a strange quiet everywhere. I kept looking around, holding my breath, waiting for something to happen. At dusk, the overseer drove by on his horse. House slaves followed in a line behind him, heads bent down. Miss Layotte looked so pale in front of him. Her collar was undone, and her apron was tied crooked.

He was the one we were waiting for, sure enough.

"Get out here!" he thundered. "Drag that old woman out of her corner too."

Everybody shot out of the cabins like mice shooting loose from their holes. Miss Layotte stepped up, and we carried Granny between us, wrapped in her woolen blanket. We set her gently down against Eliza so that it looked like she was sitting up on her own. Granny was beyond listening. No one knew it but us. If we had told just how sick and close to dying she was, they'd have ordered us not to waste our time caring for her anymore.

We all lined up like cotton plants in a straight row so that he could count us.

"From now on, no field slave allowed near the big house." He flashed his whip in front of us. "Got orders to shoot if we see you. Any of you dreamin' of a bite of food from the house, it'll be your last. Full body whippin' if you break these rules. Master's orders!"

The overseer stared at us all. One by one,

we dropped our eyes down 'cause we weren't supposed to be looking eye to eye with a white man. Then he turned straight toward my cousin.

"Think you're fit to be a nanny? Master says you're gonna be a cotton picker from tomorrow on. Even that's too good for you. Master's got plans for you. Better hide, girl!"

I heard the rushing sound of breath sucked in. Eliza's face reddened the same as if she'd been slapped. Miss Layotte shivered so beside me, I wished I was brave enough to reach out my arms and hold both girls tight.

Overseer ordered us back inside. Granny clutched onto Miss Layotte with her bony fingers as we carried her away.

"You Abram's girl?" She squinted. "The pretty one?"

Miss Layotte squeezed Granny's hand for an answer. Granny smiled sweetly back at her. She was most peaceful nowadays. Sometimes there's blessings in sorrows if you looked close enough.

"What's he tellin' you, child?" she mumbled to my cousin.

"He say," Eliza's voice was dry, shivery dry, like oak leaves rattling on a winter tree, "I got to be invisible from now on."

I was glad darkness fell early that night. I didn't want to see Eliza's face. I didn't want

161

it to hang like mine, like most slave faces, heavy with sorrows, looking older than our years.

Chapter 18

No More Sun Shine to Burn Her

It was breathless hot the next morning. No shade for miles around. That sun shone so yellow bright, there was no hiding from it. When Eliza walked across the fields, everyone rose up to witness her pass. The calico head scarf. The pale white arms and legs sticking out of her stiff burlap sack. When the crows flew by, squawking messages above her head, she didn't even look up.

I was the one chosen by the overseer to train Eliza to work cotton. That first morning, she picked by my side. Next day, she'd be on her own. Eliza studied my hands whizzing from bush to sack, how my fingertips slipped into the boll without a scratch, filling my sack brimful in a few minutes. I had nine years of picking on her. My fingers were tough as animal hide. Both my hands worked like two right hands. But that girl tore into those bolls so fast I winced.

"Pick easy, Eliza!" I warned her. "That boll's gonna dig into your skin and rip it raw. Don't matter how much you pick at first. Only matters you learn how."

Her baby-soft fingers scraped against the hard, dry boll. It hurt my ears to hear that sound. By that afternoon, she was fussing with her strap. That strap had a way of settling on the same old sore spot and rubbing away, but she didn't say a word about it.

She was not a child anymore, so no one called out, "Come girl, pick in my shadow." We picked and filled our sacks like always. We all watched Eliza though, her lips quivering like a lid on a pot that's boiling over.

But all day long, we heard the wailing. No one took care of the babies sprawled everywhere under that blasting bright sun. Those who were crawling knew just one word to call. Mom-ma! Mom-ma! But some of the older ones remembered my cousin running to 'em. E-liz-a! E-liz-a! It didn't matter what word they cried, each call was a slap on her face. My cousin picked slowly, not looking where her hands went. Her back was not straight anymore, but bent beneath the sun like the rest of us.

How the young 'uns screamed when Eliza came by at noon, clinging to her dress. She sat down on the ground and pulled 'em into her to shade them from the sun.

"Hushaby!" was all she said.

Betty passed by to drop off food. Before Eliza and their mommas got done feeding them, the conker shell blew. My cousin tiptoed away backward. Her eyes held fast on the young 'uns by the oak tree.

"Stay there, Willie!" she coaxed.

But the toddlers stumbled after her. One boy fell down and began to cry. Eliza ran back toward him. The overseer tore past us like wind, snapping his whip down against Eliza's bare arm.

"Back to the field!" he ordered her.

That first night, when Eliza laid down, she tossed this way and that, staring straight up at the ceiling. Aunt Charity came home and touched her hand light on Eliza's arms. It was flaming hot with a strawberry-red sunburn. The skin on her fingertips was raw, and her forearm was red from whipburn. My aunt patted hog grease on her skin, but Eliza jerked away, wincing.

"You chose the hard way," Aunt Charity told her, "punishin' your poor skin."

My aunt's sigh filled the room.

"All of us born into trouble on this plantation, child. For you, it's even worse. Part of me. Part of them."

"If I could just change the color of my eyes. Soon as anybody sees 'em, they know my secret. I'm half. Not whole. Half black. Half white. I don't belong to anyone."

"You belong to Aunt Charity and me!" my voice rose up.

There was a long pause. My aunt reached out her hand to Eliza.

"No easy place for you to be, is there, child?"

"Why can't I just be Eliza?" she cried. "Mindin' babies in the field. That's the place I wanna be, but they won't let me."

My aunt stroked Eliza's hair, straightening out all the tangles as if her fingers were a comb. Eliza's chest heaved like she couldn't catch her breath. Then the sobs came, hard and loud.

"I thought the world was so . . . so . . . big. Pretended something good was waitin' for me. But now I'll never be a nanny in the big house like I dreamed."

"You got a life here with us, child," Aunt Charity soothed her. "Go to the fields tomorrow and pick like nothin's happened. Everyone will soon forget about you. And cover yourself up, child."

There seemed to be no good the next day

or the next. Bright red blisters popped up on Eliza's arms and neck, and my aunt lay cool wet rags on them every night. We stopped trying to make Eliza cover up. She'd just show up in the fields each morning in her burlap sack and pick. I know how new burlap is. I won't wear it. It rubs against your skin when you sweat and chews away at it. Eliza ached from the sunburn and itched from the burlap but never said one word.

All that summer, she couldn't keep up with us. When the order came to go back to the fields after the noontime break, sometimes Eliza wouldn't hear it. She was sound asleep with the babies on her lap.

"Come a-cross, child-dren!" Ben called out to us.

"I'll take her a-cross!" I pulled my cousin to her feet.

I leaned her against me for the walk back. I wished I could hide her in the shade of the wide oak tree, wrap her in a blanket with the babies, and let her be. A whipping would come, though, if she was not where she was supposed to be.

There came a midsummer day so hot we could barely drag our feet to the fields. When we stepped into our cabin that evening, we felt a stillness, a hush, like before a summer storm. Granny did not stir in her corner. She barely moaned when we turned her over. We tried offering her a sip of water from the gourd shell, but she squeezed her mouth shut.

Next night, she lay still as death, sleeping deep, so cold to our touch. We covered her with all the blankets we could find. Aunt Charity lit a candle same as we do on birthing nights. Long before the candle dimmed, Granny was gone. But we kept it burning anyway so that she'd have light to see the way.

I looked at Granny's face sunken to bone, not scowling anymore but smooth as pond water. Granny was free. And it came to me how birth and death are two sides of a coin. One is joy. Coming in. The other is peace. Going out. The in-between is the life God gave us, a chance to find grace. Granny waited for death to find her grace. We buried her next evening beside the rock that hid her pile of silver coins. This time, when we sang, I joined in. The words rang true, through and through.

No more rain fall to wet her.
No more sun shine to burn her.
No more part-ing in the king-dom.

I walked slow after that. I thought how

168

Granny had always seen troubles first, never the blessings like my aunt. Granny felt it coming on Eliza's born day, tap-tap-tapping her boots down hard. Troubles were coming. Coming soon. Granny was right about most things. None of us wanted to believe her, most of all me.

A month later, in the bright sunlight of the fields, I noticed Eliza's blisters had all healed. Freckles dotted her cheeks and a blush sneaked up her arms and legs. From across the row, she lifted her arms high and called to the crows, teeth flashing bright white against her sun-brown face. All around us, crows rose up, screeching. *Caw! Caw! Caw!* I just shook my head. Here Eliza thought by darkening her skin, she'd be invisible. Each day, she turned browner with Cherokee red skin that shone. Her high cheekbones had a berry blush on 'em. At dusk, she glowed like a firefly. I wouldn't be the one to tell Eliza she grew prettier every day.

From across the field one day, we both saw the dust cloud blowing along the road. The black speck riding in front of it was Master's carriage. Eliza switched sides with me so her back faced the road. She picked with fierce yanking at the bushes. She never saw the carriage slow down or Miss Emma pointing Eliza out to her sister and how their heads turned to follow her for a long while down the road. Eliza did not look up. All she saw was cotton and sky.

"You puttin' those white girls behind you?" I asked her.

"Got to." She poked her fingers quick and hard into the bolls. "Everyone in the big house is against me. What I gotta do now is figure out a way for 'em to leave me be."

"Wish I could hide you, girl," I confessed. "Wrap you up tight in a thorny boll no one could pick."

Near the end of picking season, someone rode past the beaten road on his horse and halted by the edge of the field. No one paid him any mind. We were used to the overseer stopping there with a scowl, checking if we were picking fast enough. Sometimes Master stopped too, surveying his cotton. We picked through it all. This man leaned forward in his saddle to spy on us. He was a big man, dressed in a white linen suit. I remembered seeing him once before. He was strutting down that same road, close to the field where I was picking one day. He shoved a young slave girl's head to the ground.

"I own you," he had bragged, "every inch of you. You gotta do what I say even if I order you to eat this dirt here!"

He was flushed all red in the face, and I guessed right away he was drunk. White folks driving by in their carriage had turned away from him like they didn't want to see. But no one had stopped him. I remembered that too.

I was the only one who'd stared at him. The other pickers wouldn't dare raise their heads for fear the overseer would catch 'em. His face had stuck in my mind. Folks in the carriage had called him the Swedelander. They whispered about how he came from the auction that day and bought that poor girl for five hundred dollars.

I watched him through the brim of my hat, my head bent to the cotton bushes so he wouldn't notice me. Though it was mid-afternoon and so hot you could see waves of steam shiver in the air, I felt cold deep down in my bones. He was staring straight across that cotton field.

I knew right away he wanted something precious from us.

And the only precious thing we had was Eliza.

Chapter 19

Send One Angel Down

Winter came. I was too restless to play my drums. I couldn't stop shivering even when the spring sun came back. I took the lead of the hoers behind the plow then. I wore my first pair of leather boots to keep from sinking into the wet ground. There were no one's footsteps to guide me, slow me, or quicken me anymore. I had to push at the right pace, so I led and did not pull the weakest too hard, but I had to be quick enough so the overseer didn't lash us. I couldn't let anyone pass me. I leaned my chest forward and flung my hoe far ahead. I kept my eye on the plough ahead and the soil churning up deep brown behind it, weeds bending in its path.

Best thing about spring was work stopped early. Sometimes, on moonless nights, Miss Layotte and I met in the middle of the orchard, just where the peach trees ended and the apple trees began. No one could see us there. Most times, we sat back against a tree trunk, listening to the crickets and the owls. I never did say much. But one night, in May, she was already waiting for me, pacing between the rows. Her eyes were darker than the night.

She whispered to me what I'd already feared. I'd seen the crows gather in the fields the afternoon the Swedelander appeared. Swarms of 'em flew in from all over the county, spreading their wings across the sky like black storm clouds. Squawking in a hundred thunderous voices. *Caw! Caw! Caw!*

"Master's going to auction . . . he's sellin' Eliza this time!"

Something burst inside my stomach like I was gonna be sick.

"What we gonna do, Miss Layotte?" I grabbed hold of her arm.

"Don't tell your aunt," she pleaded. "Only one place to go . . . Father Johnson's . . . maybe he'll listen."

It was the name whispered at the Saturday night dance. They said he helped runaways. He bought up slaves and set 'em free too. I thought back to what Aunt Charity believed. How good comes sometimes when you're deep in troubles.

I bolted out of the quarters to Father Johnson's late that same night. The coffee-skinned man had told me his church sat high on a hill two miles past our own church, along the beaten road.

"Follow the direction of the setting sun, but wait 'til dark," he warned me. "Stay low down in the far fields by the road's edge. Don't step out 'til you come to it. Keep your ears wide open."

It was the first time I set foot outside the Turners' on a workday. Patrols roamed the road each night searching for runaways. If they found you, I had heard, they'd whip you so hard you wouldn't stand up again. I ran barefooted, barely touching the ground, traveling like wind.

There was no mistaking when I came to it. A white building reached up high to the sky, a dot of white against the night. It was a place that only white folks stepped into. I hooted three times in the bushes like Ben had taught me. That's a signal of a runaway out in the fields, he said, looking for a safe station. I wondered if my daddy hid just like me and if his heart drummed like mine. He just went ahead though. He never turned around.

When a white-haired woman lifted a candle to the night, I decided to walk up to her and show my black face. She led me into the parlor where the father was praying. I'd never spoken straight up to a white man before.

"They are selling our Eliza." The words spilled out of me soon as I saw Father Johnson's worry-worn face.

"Slow down, son," he instructed. "Tell me what happened."

"Master Turner's gonna bring my cousin to auction come the end of the month. His daughters want to get rid of her. Already some men come by to take a look at Eliza . . . one's the Swedelander."

He winced when I said that name.

"You got to save her, sir! Hide her! We can't let her be sold."

"Son, there's no use hiding her." He calmed me. "She'd have to stay hid a lifetime. We can't send her on the Underground either. They'll be watching her close, expecting her to break loose once she hears the news. But there is another way . . ."

Father Johnson laid a hand on my shoulder.

"I'll write to abolitionists up North. Maybe they'll help. If that doesn't work, we'll try to buy her ourselves."

His words were like a light blinking on in my mind.

"Son, gather what you can. I'll spread the

word at services." He grabbed my hand and shook it. "Every nickel's going to count, so that we can afford to buy Eliza her freedom at that auction."

I took in his words like grace falling down from heaven. Grace is something you wished for but never dared hope to get. I felt lighter than light. I could have lifted my wings if I had them and flew. I remembered the old green pennies I buried back of the orchard when I was a kid, how I'd been saving 'em for something. I had never known what until now. Granny too had hid silver coins. There must be plenty of 'em buried next to her.

"I'll send Mr. Lloyd by the night before the auction to collect your money," he instructed me. "Meet him under the apple trees in the orchard with three hoots just like you signaled me."

All the next day, in the field, I wondered where I should go to collect more money. Nobody dared talk about having any. At dusk, I trailed behind Ben to his cabin door and told my story.

"I'll take care of it, son," he offered right away.

"Just tell me where to run to." I yanked on his arm. "I'll go. She's my cousin."

"You're too young. Don't know your way

around these parts. You never been off this plantation. Too risky for you."

"But I ran up the hill to Father Johnson's last night!"

"If the patrol found you, they'd have left you hanging high in a tree. I got men trained to go. Never got caught yet," he explained. "They'll run to nearby plantations and into town to beg freed slaves for their coins. They know folks who'll help out."

"How will we get the money?"

"You know that old peach tree close by the quarters?" he asked. "Run by before dawn every day and pick up what they leave there. Bury it behind your cabin right away."

"Let me run with 'em," I begged again.

"Come deep dark, you'll be busy here, where folks know you," Ben ordered. "Visit each cabin. Folks heard about the auction. Word spreads fast. Some save money in secret. Maybe they'll give it to you for Eliza's sake."

Every night, for some weeks, I visited slave cabins on our plantation. Some folks I'd barely spoken one word to before, yet they knew about my cousin and me. From all hands passed pennies, quarters, and nickels, even some dollar coins pressed loose from behind a wallboard, flat into my open hand. A silver coin from a young man saving for his wedding. Quarters from a grandpa. Before first light, I checked under the peach tree and brought back what I found there to bury beneath the rock. When I walked into the cabin at dawn, Eliza was just stirring.

"Where are you runnin' every night?" she teased me. "Meetin' Miss Layotte somewhere and forgettin' all about me?"

I'd walk off, nose in the air, grinning just as if I had run off with Miss Layotte. I was thinking about what I had buried in an old flour sack, growing fatter each night beside the pile of silver coins Granny left. I could hear Granny telling me as I sunk more coins into the dirt each dawn, how money could buy a slave's freedom if you only had enough.

"If we buy her at the auction," Father Johnson had promised me, "we buy her freedom too."

Maybe that's the good that'll come out of all our troubles, I told myself.

No one told Eliza about the auction. Two nights before the auction, I walked back to the quarters to pick up the money sack for Mr. Lloyd. I made up my mind to set Eliza down for one of our evening talks and tell her what we'd planned for her. I'd show her all the money and beg her to hold on and not to worry because we'd be there.

That's when I heard the fuss. Chickens squawking. Dogs barking. Someone had passed in and out of the slave quarters fast. By the time I reached the cabin, Eliza was gone.

"They . . . they . . . took her up to the big house," sobbed my aunt. "Afraid she'd run away. Why didn't someone warn me?"

My stomach felt like it had heaved out of me and dropped down to the ground.

"He prom-ised!" My aunt pounded the ground with her bare hands. "Prom-ised I could keep my girl!"

She sat on the dirt floor with her head sunk in her hands, howling like a wild animal caught in a trap. I'd never heard anyone cry like that before. I grabbed her hands and held them to my chest. Her palms were bruised red from beating everywhere.

After a long while, she stopped and looked around the room, both of us noticing it for the first time without Eliza: the dirt floor swept flat, the window without glass, Granny's empty blanket. It seemed like it never was a home but only a shed.

Eliza was gone. We never even had a chance to tell her good-bye. At bedtime, this time of night, my cousin would have been chirping up a storm. Granny would have been fussing, trying to shush us. Soon we'd all have been rolling on the floor with laughter, paying no mind to our aching backs and growling stomachs.

In fourteen years, we had never had this kind of quiet before.

"Abram, we promised between you and me to take care of our girl," moaned my aunt, "but we just let him take her!"

I told my plan to Aunt Charity. She squeezed my hand tight, but she never rose up from the floor. I couldn't make her believe there was a way out.

That's when we both felt it. A cool breeze floating through the open door. Suddenly it was as if Eliza was all around us, whispering good-bye. I would have run up to the big house and peeked in all the windows just for a look at her, except for the freshness of that breeze, like a first spring day, Eliza's born day.

It set a calm on us.

Aunt Charity started humming and singing like old times — sweet light notes way up high. Some songs are sorrow songs and some are glory songs. And some songs, like Granny's butter song, are spell songs to chase the devil away. But I never heard a song like this one.

If-a you can't come,
If-a you can't come, Lord,
Send-a one an-gel down.
Send him on a rainbow.
Send him in a glory.
Send him in a hurry, Lord,
If-a you can't come.

This was a calling song, calling an angel down 'cause we can't do anymore. We closed our eyes and let the believing fly back into us.

When the lights dimmed in the big house, I dug beneath that rock for the last time and ran to the back of the orchard. It was deep dark. Bare branches reached toward me like bony arms. I squeezed that fat money sack tight in my fist and waited on Mr. Lloyd, hunched on my heels down in the grass. I waited a long wait. My eyes darted every which way. I rang out with three hoots, again and again.

Hours later, someone answered back with three short hoots.

"You the boy Abram that Father Johnson sent?"

"I am."

"Mr. Lloyd here." He stepped forward. "Sent to buy Eliza's freedom. If the bidding doesn't go sky-high, we can afford her. How much did you bring?"

I shrugged. Though I had touched the money and knew what each slave handed me, a quarter or a penny, I had no way of knowing how much it made all together. That night, Mr. Lloyd slipped his fingers into my sack and let the coins fall through his fingers. He mumbled something beneath his breath.

Must be counting, I guessed.

"20, 30, 40 . . . 50 dollars," he muttered to himself.

Three minutes passed, but it seemed like hours. My head kept spinning around, listening for footsteps. Finally Mr. Lloyd threw the coins back into the sack and straightened up.

"Right fine job, son," he congratulated me. "Looks to be about four hundred dollars here. Gonna make the difference between affordin' to buy Eliza or not. Father Johnson's collected a heap more."

Let it be enough, I prayed.

Chapter 20

If I Had My Way

Mr. Lloyd had told me where to find the auction block. It sat at the edge of Pott's tobacco field, he said, straight down the beaten road, three miles past the white church.

I'd heard stories about it all my life.

Granny stood in front of it once. Her grandsons had all been sold away there, one by one. She said it was where you lost somebody forever. It could be your momma or your daddy or your wife. They'd be pushed in front of a money-fisted crowd, and a white man hollered out how many sacks of cotton they picked in a day, their age, and if they were a breeder, how many children they birthed. Another man stretched their mouth wide open to show they had all their teeth. Men held the slaves down while they kicked with all their might so they wouldn't drag 'em up there. For once they did and that auctioneer slammed his hammer down and yelled "Sold!" they'd be gone.

I didn't show up to work in the fields on the day of Eliza's auction. I didn't care if I got a full-body whipping for it. Ben planned to space the cotton hoers in the field so that it would look like no one was missing. A woman from the fields, full hipped enough to be my aunt, took over her job tending the breeding cabins. We spent the night before full awake. Aunt Charity tore away at her hair, while I paced the dirt floor.

The next morning, we slipped out of the cabin before sunup. We ran like rabbits through the woods alongside the beaten road. Every once in a while, I peeked out to see. By daybreak, we passed Father Johnson's. Later, when the south wind blew the scent of sun-dry tobacco our way, I knew I was at Pott's field. We crept through the tobacco plants on our hands and knees, snuggling down deep in the rows to wait on Eliza.

Even hiding in the bushes, I could smell that block. Pinewood was hammered high above the ground into a platform, so that everyone could get a look even standing in the back of a crowd. The platform was weathered some, turning gray in the sun, with a streak of red running down its steps. Slave's blood.

One of Granny's grandchildren had kicked up such a storm when he was being sold that the overseer had shot him. He swore he'd just meant to knick his ear, but the bullet sunk into his head instead.

"At least he's not sold," Granny had told me, "to a mean master to be worked to death. He's gone, but we know where he's at. Sleepin' deep at the back of the orchard. Gone to God."

I remembered a song she had sung about Samson, the strongest man. He had lost his strength and freedom both. He'd prayed to God to give his strength back to him one more time so that he could tumble down the building where he was enslaved. I wished for the same, watching and waiting by the auction block.

> *If I had my way,*
> *I'd tear this build-ing down.*
> *If I had my way.*

Round noon, the crowd showed up. I seen 'em with my own eyes. White folks from town, with nothing to do, dressed up fine and spinning umbrellas in the air like they were going to a dance. Most of 'em came to get an eyeful, not to buy.

My aunt and I squatted close together. We didn't dare whisper. Just listened is all. Horses' hooves shook the ground beneath us. Wagon wheels screeched to a halt. We both stretched our heads up. An overseer snapped his whip against a wagon. A slave's head popped up from the back. He had been sitting tight in a ball beside a female slave, but now he stepped down one foot at a time, both hands tied tight behind his back. Though he was over six foot tall with a broad bare chest, he kept his head down, so he looked small. He followed the overseer to the platform like his shadow.

But our eyes were not on him. We kept searching the wagon, trying to see the one slave hidden there.

"This here is Silas," announced the auctioneer. "Picks four hundred pounds of cotton in a day. Won't find a stronger man."

"Six hundred!" one plantation owner called out immediately.

"Seven!" yelled another man in a striped suit.

Silas did not move. Only his eyes followed each bidder. Soon his face began to twitch as he stood in front of the crowd.

"Eight!" someone called out.

"Eight hundred and fifty!" shouted a voice from the back.

"One thousand!" the man in the striped suit yelled.

The crowd looked all around for another bid. Umbrellas twirled in the sun. Rivers of sweat dripped down Silas's chest.

"Sold for one thousand dollars to Master Carter!"

The overseer pushed Silas down the platform steps toward his new owner. The last I saw of the slave was his shiny bare back, rippled with scar marks from old whippings.

The auctioneer's hammer hit down so hard, I jumped. When I looked up, a female slave had already been shoved onto the platform. My aunt leaned out of the bushes to see if she was Eliza.

"Sally's twenty-two years old. Birthed three babies. Ready for more."

The slave paced the platform like she would have jumped off if a group of white men weren't standing on all sides below her. Her hair was undone and waved wildly in her face. She searched through the crowd with wide, dark eyes.

"Four hundred!" an offer began.

"Some of you gentlemen need a woman to tend your babies?" the auctioneer offered.

"Sally's trained as a wet nurse. Birthed her last child two months ago."

A baby cried out from the back, a long wail. Sally froze and turned in its direction. An overseer's wife held a black baby in her arms, trying to shush it.

"All her babies healthy too!" the auctioneer said.

Heads turned. A few low laughs broke out over the crowd.

"Six hundred!" The bid continued.

"Seven!"

"Seven hundred and fifty!"

The bids called out from every corner, but Sally paid no attention to 'em. She leaned off the edge of the auction block. White men held her ankles tightly down to the platform.

"One thousand!"

"Thirteen hundred!"

"Thirteen hundred and fifty dollars!"

Silence. All eyes watched the auctioneer while he scanned the crowd.

"Sold to Master Cohoon for thirteen hundred and fifty!"

White men yanked Sally away from the platform, but she would not budge. Some yanked her arms and others shoved her legs. She screamed and kicked her way through the crowd.

"Give me back my baby!" we heard her cry.

In a few minutes, Sally passed out of the crowd. Folks talked and laughed for a time. The auctioneer was quiet. My aunt held her hands to her chest and closed her eyes, but I was drenched in sweat. I kept worrying where Eliza was, wondering if they took her elsewhere to be sold, when suddenly the voices died down. When I peeked out, all heads were turned toward the road. Master Turner stepped up with Miss Abigail prancing beside him like a prize pony. There was no sign of Miss Emma or her momma. Behind them, a cloud of dust kicked up.

It was Eliza.

She came wrapped in a rope tied to the overseer's horse, and she came fighting. She fought to stay standing too, twisting this way and that when the overseer yanked at that rope.

The crowd of white folks fell back. The overseer shoved Eliza up on that platform with her back to us. I saw what he did. Dressed her up in a red silk dress and bonnet. He stripped that dress down so everyone could see Eliza's long bare back, shining white as bone in the sun.

Aunt Charity pushed my head down into the bushes. But I heard that crowd admiring Eliza.

Words buzzed like a thousand mosquitoes.

Then it rose, louder than the crowd, a mournful wailing.

Came the voice I knew even in my sleep.

Eliza screamed out, "Leave me be!"

"Shut up," Overseer barked, "or I'll knock your brains out, girl!"

Bang! The hammer slammed down so hard, it shook the ground I was lying on.

"Look up here!" the auctioneer called out. "A lively mulatto girl. Fifteen years old. A beauty. And a trained nanny too. Bidding starts at eight hundred dollars. Who will offer me the first bid?"

"I'll take her for one thousand dollars!" shouted a deep voice.

I popped my head up. It was the Swedelander, swaying back and forth on his feet. His suit was all smeared with mud like he'd spent the night in a ditch.

"Twelve hundred!" announced a smooth, crisp voice.

It was a stranger. He stood by himself in the crowd, feet planted wide apart, dressed in a silver waistcoat. His boots were polished. His shirt was so white, it gleamed like a full moon. He didn't draw his words out long like Master but clipped 'em short. Must be a gentleman from the North. Master Turner studied him from head to toe and nodded to his daughter. Miss Abigail twirled her parasol in the sun like she was at a courting party.

"Thirteen hundred for the girl!" rang another voice.

I sat straight up to listen. It was Mr. Lloyd, dressed in a suit too big for him, hanging loose and torn at the elbows.

"What may your interest be, sir?" demanded the auctioneer. "You're no plantation owner. Not a rich man either by the looks of you."

Mr. Lloyd cleared his throat and swallowed hard.

"Good folks have raised enough money to buy this slave."

Eliza slowly turned her head toward the tobacco plants. She stared down row after row.

"What folks? Name them!"

"Good sir!" protested Mr. Lloyd. "I am sworn to secrecy."

Heads turned. Voices rose, complaining like crows. Master Turner raised his fist at Mr. Lloyd and marched straight to the platform. The auctioneer wiped sweat off his bald head and stepped down to talk to someone holding all the money and the slaves' papers. He sat with a fat cigar stuck in his mouth. He was the sheriff. I'd seen him at the big house before, laughing with

Master. He motioned the auctioneer to bang his hammer down.

"Listen here, man! Your money is no good in the South," he shouted. "It's probably slave money. Who knows where they got it from! Stealin', no doubt. You got plans to set her free? We sell slaves for hire, not freedom. Clear out or I'll have you arrested for stealin'."

Master Turner set his thumbs in his waistcoat and stuck his chest out like a pigeon. I wished for a fistful of mud to throw at him. Mr. Lloyd wrung his hands and hung his head. A group of deputies shoved him through the crowd with the butt of their shotguns, and he was gone. My aunt and I sunk flat down in the grass, closed our eyes, and clung tight together.

"Let's get back down to business," we heard the auctioneer announce from the platform. "I got an offer of twelve hundred dollars from — where are you from, good sir?"

"New York," came the answer.

"The man from New York offers twelve hundred for this fine mulatto," he reminded the crowd. "Who will raise him?"

"Fifteen hundred!" yelled the Swedelander, red in the face, staring at the man from New York.

"Eighteen hundred!" the cool, crisp voice of the man from New York rang out.

"What you gonna do with this slave if you buy her?" the Swedelander laughed at the stranger. "You're no plantation owner. You gonna carry her all the way to New York?"

"None of your business what I do with this girl," the man faced him square, "but you don't have money enough to buy her."

The Swedelander's big mouth opened wide, and we all heard, "Two thousand."

The words hung on the air, neither of us wanting to believe in 'em. Master Turner grinned like a cat. Overseer slammed his hands against his legs like he had heard a joke. Eliza was standing stiff as a tree up on that auction platform. But Aunt Charity pressed her hands over her ears, worry lines spread over her face like a million roads.

Nobody spoke. Nobody breathed.

All eyes landed on the man from New York.

I stared at him like I was trying to see through his white skin. Words pounded inside me as loud as my heartbeat.

"Please sir, please don't let Eliza be sold to that Swedelander. He's gonna use her all up. Please, please, sir, buy her right now with all the money you got!"

Beside me, I heard the low moaning and

whispering of my aunt praying for Eliza. It sounded like buzzing bees. I was afraid she was going to shout to God like she does in church. She squeezed my hands so tight, I almost hollered out.

Seconds ticked by. Then we all heard "Twen-ty-five hun-dred dol-lars!"

The man from New York said it slow and loud, pronouncing each single letter like it was his last.

The Swedelander's turn was next.

It was real quiet. Nobody moved. The Swedelander turned something purple in the face. He dug his hands deep into his pockets, fingering his money. Big drops of sweat darkened the back of his suit. He squeezed his fist and raised it up like he was gonna hit the man from New York, but he just sent it flying in the air so it didn't hit anybody but his own leg. Then he straightened himself up and walked off.

We stretched up high to watch him go. We couldn't help staring. It was like the devil himself had lost at his favorite game.

Slam! The hammer hit down hard.

"Sold!" the auctioneer yelled. "For twenty-five hundred dollars, to the man from New York!"

Chapter 21

A Band of Angels Coming After Her

Eliza stumbled down the steps of the auction block with the sheriff's men at her heels. Master Turner stood watching, with his legs planted wide apart, a fat cigar stuck in his mouth. Smoke curled around him like he stood in hell. In the bushes, my aunt and I lay flat on the ground, curled into one another. Her hand was in mine, cold and limp as if her heart had stopped.

The men dragged Eliza in front of the man from New York.

"Eliza." He looked down at her papers. "Is that your name?"

"Yes, sir."

I stared through the bushes. Eliza faced him straight same as she looks at us, not shamed or fretting like I would be to look a white man in the eye.

"I just signed your papers, Eliza. You are free from now on."

Aunt Charity suddenly stirred. She lifted to her knees and peeked out.

"Good sir . . . what . . . are you saying!" Master Turner butted his way through the crowd.

He stood face to face with the man from New York.

"Abolitionists in the North told me of these cursed auctions," he answered. "Sent me here. Raised money to buy one slave's freedom today. No matter what the cost."

"You can't walk in here to buy a slave and set her free!" Master Turner whirled around. "Tell him so, sheriff."

The sheriff loosened his collar.

"Man paid cash. More than you hoped for. Auction's over. Paper's already signed."

"But you banned Mr. Lloyd!"

"He's one of us Southerners. Nobody's gonna fight for him here," insisted the sheriff. "This man's from the North. Backed by some antislavery society. Bring us plenty of trouble if we stop him."

"But he's settin' her free!" Master screamed.

"It's his property to do with as he sees fit. He done bought her."

The sheriff headed back to the auction

block with his men. He motioned the crowd to head back to town. Master Turner stared after him with such a hanging of his jaw that his cigar fell out. He jammed his money into his pocket and stomped off. Miss Abigail flushed red in the face. She marched behind her father, stabbing her parasol into the ground with each and every step. Don't know where the overseer went. He disappeared like smoke.

The man from New York watched the crowd leave. He looked at his watch and cleared his throat.

"Eliza, you are free," we heard him announce. "Nobody can stop you now that I signed. You can go now."

My aunt and I squeezed our hands tight. We studied each other's face to see if we had heard right.

"Free? . . . I am free!"

Eliza twirled around and around, lifting her face up to the heavens that made her, so I knew she was thanking somebody and that would be God. When she came to a stop, her eyes set on the man from New York.

"But sir . . . what will I do now? Where will I go?"

"There must be some freed slaves living in town." He walked toward his carriage. "Go there. Get a job."

197

"Sir, I can't go to town! They'd hunt me down. They'd never let me live free." Eliza's voice quivered. "That . . . man will find me."

The next thing I knew, my aunt twisted her hand out of mine and jumped out of the tobacco bushes. I stayed still, stayed down low, waiting for some commotion. There was a rumble far off of wagon wheels rolling away.

My aunt's voice rang across the field, clear as a crow.

"You got a family who loves you, sir?"

"Why, yes, I do," the man from New York answered politely, "at my home in New York City."

"Who may they be?" Aunt Charity's voice lifted higher.

"My wife. Three children. Another child to be born soon."

"Who's takin' care of 'em, sir?" demanded my aunt.

"My own good wife, a minister's daughter. She's used to working hard."

"She's gonna need someone to help her now," announced my aunt. "Four children soon, and her husband a travelin' man. Eliza's good with children. Trained by our granny and a Creole nanny both."

A silence came. I lifted my head then, so the sun fell on me. It lit me up like a target, but I didn't care anymore. I scanned the field in all directions. There was no one left but us. The gentleman and my aunt faced each other. A few feet away, my cousin stood motionless. I stretched full up and ran to my aunt's side. The gentleman looked away from us, yanking at his tie.

"I can't take her!" he insisted. "I just paid plenty to set her free. We don't believe in slaves up North. We —"

"She won't come as a slave, sir," interrupted my aunt. "She'll be your children's own nanny if you give her a home. Someplace safe."

The gentleman stepped back some from us. But now my cousin stirred. She rushed up close to him and stood between him and his carriage.

"Eliza, take your freedom!" he commanded her. "I got business to attend to."

The man from New York tipped his hat and turned away. Eliza spun like a whirlwind, her skirts flying until she landed square in front of the white man, the brim of her hat touching his. Her back pressed flat against his carriage, blocking the way.

He couldn't pass us by. All three of us stared at him like we were one person.

"All my life, I been trainin' for one thing," Eliza spoke up. "To be a nanny. Can't be anything else. You have set me free. There's only one place I can go — to New York with you."

Eliza's eyes lit on the man from New York like she'd never let him go. At last, the gentleman turned to Aunt Charity.

"Are you willing for this child of yours to go to New York?"

"If she is free and no one ever owns her again . . . yes!"

She whispered so soft, it was hard to hear her.

The man from New York looked at Aunt Charity and me.

"Wish I could afford to take you all back," he sighed.

The man from New York looked into the distance. There came such a stillness then. I turned around to see if we were still safe. Not one person remained in the field.

"I will take one of you back," he announced. "Eliza! She'll be as free as I am. If she doesn't like the job, she can work elsewhere, I promise you. All she has to do is work hard."

"Eliza's used to that." Aunt Charity's voice rose up.

That's when the man from New York handed Eliza a yellowed paper.

"You must carry this wherever you go,

Eliza. The law can ask you for it anytime. Once we get to New York, you'll be safe."

Eliza reached out for those papers, her eyes wide and blue as morning sky, touching the words with her fingers as if to make them real. Aunt Charity studied that paper close, looking at the words no slave could read.

"It says," the man from New York read over our shoulders, "that one Eliza, born on Turner plantation in the state of Alabama, is free from the age of fifteen, on this day, June 29, 1860."

Aunt Charity folded herself into Eliza. She petted her hair just like I had seen her do that morning in the breeding cabin some fifteen years ago. She stroked her head from top to shoulders, stretching out her long hair like wings.

"Got us a girl child, isn't she a beauty?"

Aunt Charity whispered it over and over again, so that, if I closed my eyes, I'd be flying back to Eliza's born day, hearing the flapping of two crows overhead announcing good luck for a girl child born a slave.

"Go now, child," she said at last.

My aunt kissed my cousin and stepped back. Tears poured down her face, but she was smiling right through them like sun peeking out of clouds.

Eliza wiped her eyes with the back of her

hand. She slipped that paper up her sleeve and straightened up.

"I am ready, sir."

"Come along then," he ordered. "We are bound for New York."

Eliza hugged her momma tight one last time, and then she reached out her hand to me, and I grabbed it hard as I could, not wanting to ever let it go. Maybe I even pulled her back some, back to the South with me. For long minutes, everything stood still. Nobody moved. Just Eliza and me holding hands.

I opened my mouth to speak, but the words ached in my throat. I had to take a deep breath before pushing my words out.

"You born for freedom, girl."

"I can't say good-bye. You're such a part of me, Abram. Gonna think of you takin' care of my momma for me."

I felt Aunt Charity's hands smoothing down my curls.

Everything began to stir then. The gentleman's horses stomped their hooves and neighed, restless to run back to New York. I swallowed hard to keep the tears down. I hugged my cousin tight one last time before she walked away.

"Tell the crows I am free, Abram!" she called back to me.

Eliza stepped into a carriage with her bonnet lifted high and rode off with the man from New York. Aunt Charity and I locked our hands tightly together and sank back down into the bushes to wait on nightfall. We watched the road until we couldn't see 'em anymore, until the sky turned pink, then grew dark.

It was safe to go back then, to slip through the woods, not saying one word. Everything felt different, like we were the only folks left in the world. The air felt soft around us, gentle, like a spring storm had ended.

At the edge of the quarters, something stirred. A field worker stepped out from behind a tree. He led us to Ben's cabin. Folks were waiting there to hear the news.

"She's gone," whispered my aunt in a hollow voice.

An old woman walked over and put her hands on Aunt Charity's shoulders. But I stood tall and lifted my head up.

"She left with her freedom papers," I told them, "and a job in New York."

Folks gasped. Some shook my hand. Ben grinned from ear to ear. All the while, my aunt leaned against me heavy as a fallen tree.

Finally she turned to Ben and sighed.

"What we gonna sing for my girl? Got to sing something, or I'm gonna set right down here and not get up again."

"Got to be a sad song," offered a mother.

"Ain't got no song for freedom," a field slave muttered.

But the old woman insisted, "Got to be a glory song!"

"There's one we all know," decided Ben. "Farewell song. Got sadness and glory both."

Ben was already humming the tune low. Folks sang in a whisper so that no one would hear us. I lifted my voice with theirs.

> *I looked over Jor-dan*
> *And what did I see?*
> *A band of an-gels com-ing af-ter me,*
> *Com-ing for to car-ry me home.*
> *Swing now, sweet cha-ri-ot,*
> *Com-ing for to car-ry me home.*

We walked back home to our cabin, still singing. Aunt Charity stumbled so slow, bent over like Granny, barely humming. I led her inside, folded her into the burlap, and rocked her back and forth. I smoothed her hair down with my hands like she'd done with mine a hundred times.

I promised her as she shut her eyes,

A band of an-gels coming after her,
Com-ing for to car-ry her home.

She soon was silent as a sleeping bird. To-morrow I would coax her to tie her hair up in rags and sing the angel song to me again. Tomorrow.

There was not one sound in that empty cabin. But inside me was thunder and rain banging to get out. I just had to scream somewhere, with all that black sky above me, where no one could hear. Scream from my gut all the worries I'd been storing up these fifteen years. Holler out loud: E-liz-a!

I grabbed my drums and ran. I ran hard 'til I couldn't breathe anymore. In the middle of the orchard, I squatted down and pounded. It was the only thing I knew to do. Wind blew. Trees waved bare branches like arms trying to touch the sky. It was a good night for sending messages.

Hear me Eliza, I beat.

At first, the pounding was hard, the flesh of my palms smacked down against the tight skin. Hear me Eliza! Faster and faster my palms beat. My hands seemed to slam down by themselves for a long while, and then they slowed down.

When I looked up, the moon hung right above my head, brightening the orchard white as snow. I remembered Jonah. How he watched and waited for his chance to get out. Plotted deep in the belly of the whale. Never gave up. I knew without a doubt that, if someone rolled around in that belly with him, someone he loved, he'd push her out first.

My arms were heavy from drumming, but I felt light, so light, as if I could fly over the miles and whisper to Eliza in her carriage headed north, "Wherever you are girl, I am still with you."

And then I saw her, dressed in long skirts, tiny waist. The scent of roses bloomed all around me. I didn't know how long she was standing there. She was leaning against a peach tree, tears running down her face. She stirred when I called and knelt down beside me. I reached up my arms, folded myself into Miss Layotte's skirts and finally cried. I hung on like I never hung on to anybody before.

I shut my eyes tight. Faces passed by in my mind. Granny smiling at me, her face smooth as pond water. Eliza's round, light-brown cheeks. And then the face of someone I never met, a young woman who looked like Eliza. She had blue eyes and was thin as a willow reed. She ran her fingers through my hair and rocked me in her arms at last.

"Hush-a-by, A-bram!" she sang. "Don't you cry!"

I knew where I was at — visiting my momma in a place that glowed like moonlight.

When finally I opened my eyes, Miss Layotte was smiling down at me. She leaned close and brushed her lips against my cheek. A kiss as soft as down feathers fluttering. I let loose a sigh. I must have been holding my breath ever since I met that girl.

"Come morning," I promised her, "I'm gonna do as Eliza asked. Wake the crows up with all my shoutin'. Scream to 'em what happened to Eliza so they can squawk the news all over the cotton fields!"

I knew how I'd walk to the fields next morning too: head straight up, back like a ramrod weed poking out of the ground, eyes on the sky, scouting for two crows to fly by overhead.

But there'll be no more tears for Eliza. There is one of us free.

And that is my cousin, Eliza.

Afterword

Abram* was freed from slavery, along with all slaves, after the Civil War ended, in December 1865. It is not known whether he ever saw his cousin Eliza again. However, when he was interviewed as an old man and ex-slave in 1930 by the Federal Writers' Project, his strongest memory was that of his cousin Eliza, for that was the story he told them.

*Abram is a pseudonym for Doc Daniel Dowdy.

Author's Note

I first began to explore slavery as a fourth-grade classroom teacher in New York City. Our social studies curriculum covered the history of New York City, and that included slavery. The first slave arrived in New York in 1626. Slavery existed in the North and not just the South. No one stopped it for a long time. When I discussed slavery with my class, their faces were blank. "What was it like to be a slave?" they asked me.

I had not experienced it. How could I teach them about it?

Literature changed me. I read Alex Haley's *A Different Kind of Christmas* in one day and stayed awake all night, the horror of slavery pressing on me like a heavy weight. By the next morning, my mind was full of the words and faces of slaves. I wondered how I could share my reaction with children in words they would understand. I discovered Eloise Greenfield's poem, "Harriet Tub-man," from *Honey I Love*. The children were amazed to learn of the secret passage to

Canada called the Underground Railroad, a trip Tubman traveled nineteen times. The awe of one slave's bravery shivered through them. We memorized and acted out that poem again and again.

A single book, *To Be A Slave*, by Julius Lester, became a bible in our study of slavery. It contains quotes from actual slaves. In the words of an ex-slave, "If you want Negro history, you will have to get it from somebody who wore the shoe." The children and I sat in a circle on the floor as I read it aloud. They held their breath listening to the words of ex-slaves who were interviewed by the Federal Writers' Project in the 1930s. The slaves spoke to us about their ancestors being torn away from Africa, dying in the middle passage across the ocean, and their abuse working on plantations in America. Their stories made us feel as if we were there. My students shed tears, and so did I. The slaves' voices remained inside me when I sat down to write *Send One Angel Down*.

It was in *To Be A Slave* that I first read about Eliza. For five years, her story haunted me. Eliza's life was turned around in one moment. That seemed like a miracle. I began to write my novel to explore what helped Eliza change her fate that day. I started with a birth scene. The situation we are born into often determines and limits our life: Eliza was born to a slave mother, so she became a slave too. The story could have ended there, but it didn't. Eliza was loved and mentored by her family. Although he couldn't free her, Abram softened the effects of slavery and fatherlessness on his cousin. Granny and Miss Layotte prepared Eliza to be independent, and Aunt Charity taught her to be hopeful. Then the man from New York, an abolitionist, showed up at the auction one day and bought Eliza's freedom. Chance is no accident. It finds us when we are ready. By the day of the auction, Eliza not only had inner strength, but she had trained as a nanny. She was prepared on that day to move beyond the chains of slavery. It was no chance. It was grace.

I searched for a way to describe the slaves' inner lives. There is a language that rolls together poetry, history, and feeling, and that language is music. It is the voice of the soul. Slaves compressed their fears, longings, and joys into one of the few outlets they were allowed: song. They sang everywhere: in the cotton fields, churning butter, at births and funerals. As a child, I remember my mother singing black folksongs, worksongs, lullabies, and spirituals. I did not know what the songs meant, but I felt the deep emotion they expressed.

In my search for songs to mirror Abram's and Eliza's experiences, I am indebted to the Central Library of the Queens Borough Public Library for their collection of songs from slavery days. By the 1940s, researchers were making efforts to collect such songs. Many songs of slavery were disappearing by then; they had only existed in the oral tradition of small Southern communities. Another rich source of song was listening to "Wade in the Water," an audiohistory series of African-American song, compiled by Dr. Bernice Johnson Regan and made available through the Smithsonian Institute. In that series, I first learned of all the angel songs originating during slavery. It compelled me to search for more. I found "Send One Angel Down" in an old book from 1925, *Mellows*, by Emmet Kennedy. It gave words to the unspoken prayers of Abram and his aunt.

For use of their extensive archives on black history, I am indebted to the Schomburg Center for Research in Black Culture of the New York Public Library System and the Langston Hughes Community Library and Cultural Center of the Queens Borough Public Library System.

As I was completing this novel, I heard ex-slaves tell their stories in an audio/book collection, *Remembering Slavery*, also based on the Federal Writers' Project from the 1930s. It was in their voices, old and thin, full of suffering and fierce strength, that my students and I could finally imagine what it was like to be a slave.

	DATE DUE		